The Soldiers of Wrath: Grit Chapter

Sam Crescent and Jenika Snow

KING (The Soldiers if Wrath: Grit Chapter)
Sam Crescent and Jenika Snow
http://www.CrescentSnowPublishing.com
Published by Crescent Snow Publishing
Copyright © April 2016 by Sam Crescent and Jenika Snow
Digital Edition
First E-book Publication: April 2016

EROTIC ROMANCE AUTHORS

CRESCENT
SNOW

Other titles by Crescent Snow Publishing

Cocky (A Taboo Short)

King has always lived his life the way he saw fit and didn't care what anyone thought. Women were just a passing hobby to waste time and warm his bed. Being the VP of the Soldiers of Wrath Grit Chapter meant he had other responsibilities and priorities besides taking up with an old lady. But then Clara came into town and something shifted in him. For the first time in his life he felt possessive and territorial of a female. It felt damn good, but it also messed with his head, especially when she claims to want nothing more from him aside from the monster he's packing behind his fly.

Clara won't ever settle down, and no man will ever own her. Visiting a friend in Grit, she discovers King, a man who refuses to back down. All she wants is to have some fun and to save enough money to move onto the next town, the next adventure. Every time she tries to get away, King is there, giving her a reason to stay. What will she do when King makes her realize she's falling in love? Can she trust him with her heart? What happens when she does try to run?

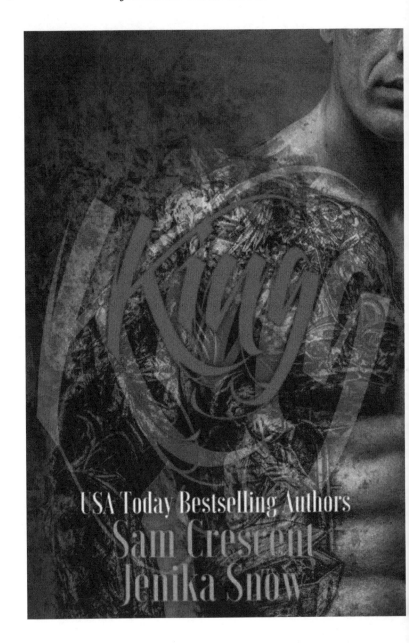

King

USA Today Bestselling Authors
Sam Crescent
Jenika Snow

Chapter One

King stared at the club whore sucking his cock, and he gripped her head, forcing her to take every single inch of him. He held onto her hair, making her take him to the back of her throat. She relaxed, accepting him. Using her mouth as a cunt, he fucked her lips, not caring as saliva dripped down the length of his dick, coating his balls. They were behind the clubhouse in Grit. They had just come back from another gun run, and the party was in full swing.

He'd grabbed the first woman he'd seen naked and had started to fuck her face. This whore knew what to do with her mouth, and he was more than happy to fill it with his spunk. Once he was done with her mouth, he was going to go and grab himself a beer.

"Fuck, baby, that's right, suck my dick, swallow it down." He pumped into her mouth, not caring about being gentle as she took all of him. Closing his eyes, he fucked her hard, and his balls tightened. Spilling his cum into her mouth, King smirked as the bitch swallowed and gagged. They were all greedy bitches, and that was exactly why he loved club whores.

There was not a single woman in the club that didn't want to spread their legs for them. They fucking loved getting cock, and he and his club brothers were more than ready to give them all the dick they could handle.

Once she was done, King tucked himself back in his pants and walked away.

"What about me?" the bitch asked.

He didn't even know her name, nor did he care to. "Fuck no. Take care of yourself."

Grim and Reaper were laughing as he walked past them.

"What the fuck are you laughing at?" King asked.

"You've just won me a hundred bucks," Reaper said, holding his hand out to Grim.

"Fucker! Why couldn't you just give her an orgasm?" Grim asked, handing the money over to his friend.

"You bet on me?" he asked.

"You're the one brother who is known to leave the women begging for a big fat O." Reaper chuckled. "And I'm always profiting from it."

"Why can't you just finger them?" Grim asked. "The past month I've lost over a thousand dollars because of you."

Grim stormed off.

"They're not our women."

"Have you heard the way Bridget is howling because of Beast?"

He had heard the woman that Beast had claimed as his old lady a couple of months ago. She wasn't exactly quiet when she came. There were moments in the middle of the night when he was lying on his bed, and he'd hear the echo of her pleasure through the walls of the clubhouse. That was the hardest.

Beast looked so damn happy with himself and had been since Bridget was in his life. King had never thought of a woman making a guy happy. He'd seen couples during his many travels, and he found most relationships lacking.

"I'm not the bitch's boyfriend," he said, storming into the clubhouse. He was now pissed off, and he didn't understand it. The orgasm that he had just experienced no longer relaxed him.

Slamming his hand down on the bar, he ordered a beer. Glancing out at the room, he watched the party going on. Men and women wrapped around each other, fucking and having fun. In the corner, he saw Beast had Bridget pinned against the wall.

Taking the bottle, he drank down nearly half before turning his attention back to the bar.

Payne took a seat beside him with a blonde bitch on his arm. "I heard Grim got rich again because of you."

"It's no one's fucking business but mine."

His Prez smirked, dipping his hand between the woman's thighs that stood beside him. "You just don't understand how to stroke a woman. Take Vicky here." Prez lifted up her skirt. "Her pussy is all nice and wet and ready for cock, but there's a way to make her do whatever the hell I want." King sat down, figuring he may enjoy the show. Payne was known for playing with his women. "Open your thighs, baby."

Vicky spread her legs, and King caught sight of her naked, wet cunt.

Payne stroked over her clit and started to nibble on Vicky's neck. King watched as she closed her eyes, reaching to grab Payne's cock and start to rub his dick. "You see, King, the reason you want to learn to give a woman what she needs, you get so much better from her. Vicky's going to get wetter, her cunt softer, and she's going to ride my cock just so she can get a second orgasm." Payne slid a finger inside her, and King's cock twitched as the woman started getting off on it. He pulled his fingers from her pussy, teasing her clit, then sliding back down to enter two fingers this time. Vicky moaned, rocking on Payne's fingers. She also had her hand inside Payne's pants and was working over his cock.

"Please, Payne, please," Vicky said, begging.

"What you're doing by ignoring the women's needs, King, is failing yourself. You're not getting the chance to know what a nice warm cunt really feels like." Payne wasn't done there. He pulled Vicky off him, and there at the bar, Payne removed his pants, tore into a condom, and placed the latex over his dick. He grabbed Vicky and slowly lowered her over his large cock. King swallowed more of his beer as he watched Vicky's face become a mask of ecstasy. When Payne was seated deep inside her, he went back to stroking Vicky's clit. "Now is where teasing a woman really works out well for us. Look at her, King, look at how she's riding my dick and loving every second of it."

King watched as Payne fucked Vicky in front of him. He saw the way Vicky was riding Payne, giving herself over to the pleasure that their Prez was giving to her. King knew most of the club whores wanted Payne's attention, as he was known for being one of the best in bed.

When Vicky screamed her release, the room erupted.

Payne didn't stop, he kept on fucking her, and only when she came twice more did he let her go.

"That's how it's done," Payne said, picking Vicky up and walking away with his cock still covered with the used condom.

Clara stared at the clubhouse and sighed. Vicky had invited her to their party, and she couldn't believe she was even here. Stepping up to the front door, she noticed two men were leaned against the wall, smoking and getting their dicks sucked by scantily-clad women at the same time. They were smiling and laughing as if they weren't getting blow jobs.

Shaking her head, she made her way toward the front door, but when one of the men shouted at her, she turned toward them.

"What are you doing here?" the one on the right asked.

"I was invited. It's a club party, right?"

"Who invited you?" This came from the one on the left.

"Vicky. She's a club girl." She didn't feel comfortable referring to her friend as a club whore even though Vicky didn't mind. When she last talked to Vicky, her friend had been so excited as she caught the eye of the club Prez, which was some big deal apparently. From the way Vicky sounded it was like she'd been picked to fuck a movie star or something.

"Grim," the one on the left said.

"Excuse me?" Clara said.

"That's my name. This is Reaper," Grim said, pointing to the other man.

"Am I not allowed in the club?" she asked.

"Are you part of any other club?" Reaper asked.

"No. I'm just a friend of Vicky's. I don't live in Grit, though. I'm just passing through. I'm at the hotel just off the main road. Vicky said it would be fine for me to stop here."

Both men pushed the women off their dicks and tucked themselves away. "We'll show you in."

She frowned at how excited the men seemed to be, and she wasn't just talking about their dicks. They moved to her sides, both of them wrapping an arm around her back. Neither of them frightened her as she had a feeling they were up to something that had nothing to do with her. But it was a little awkward the way they were so forward.

They entered the clubhouse and she wasn't surprised by the state of undress and fucking that was going on. She'd been travelling a lot the past five years, and she'd seen a hell of a lot more than this debauchery. Clara wasn't a prude by any means.

"What the fuck are you two doing now?" A large man stood up from the bar. He looked pissed, and his hair was slicked back and fell to his neck.

"She's Vicky's friend. We're going to take her to see her."

"You know he doesn't like being interrupted."

"Doesn't matter. King, are you coming?"

Before she could say anything, she was being led away toward the back of the clubhouse and up several flights of stairs. She didn't put up a fight as she'd not even seen Vicky yet.

"What's your name?" the man they'd called King, asked.

"Clara."

He grunted. "I'm King, and I'm sure you were already introduced to these two fuckers," he said, pointing to Grim and Reaper.

"He's going to be so pissed."

"And it's fucking funny," Reaper said.

"You two have a death wish," King said.

They came to a stop, and Clara rolled her eyes at the clear sound of Vicky in orgasm. She had heard it enough during their twenty-year friendship to know when Vicky was getting off. They had met when they were five years old and had only parted ways when they were twenty but stayed in touch. Clara had left to spread her wings, and Vicky stayed in Grit. Clara had no reason to settle down and stay in town, and so she went on the road, exploring everything that life had to offer.

Without knocking, Grim opened the door, and Clara sighed. Vicky was on her hands and knees on the bed, and a very large, muscular man was fucking her from behind. This was not the first time she'd seen her friend in such a position.

Folding her arms, she watched the man fucking Vicky. He glared at them before throwing a book that was on a shelf bedside him.

"I'm not in the mood to be watched right now. Get the fuck out."

Vicky squealed, turned her head, and Clara laughed when she saw the recognition in her friend's eyes.

"Clara, you made it."

"You did tell me to be here by nine, and guess what, Vicky, it's nine." Clara tapped her watch.

"Shit, sorry." Vick tapped Payne's thigh. "Payne, this is my friend, the one I was telling you about, Clara."

Payne had paused inside Vicky.

"Hi, Payne," Clara said.

"Clara. We're a little busy. You think you can keep yourself entertained?"

"I certainly can," Clara said. Before she walked away, she entered the room and went to her friend. It had been over a year since she'd seen Vicky.

"What the fuck are you doing?" Payne asked.

She wrapped her arm around Vicky's back, kissing her head. Strange as it was to do this right now, he'd seen Vicky in a hell of a lot of compromising positions. She didn't care. Vicky, in turn hugged her back.

"I missed you, honey," Clara said.

"I missed you too. You're going to love it here."

"I can imagine." Clara gave Payne a smile. "See you soon." Clara left them alone and closed the door behind her.

"Where the fuck did you come from?" Grim asked.

"Nowhere."

"Oh fuck, will you marry me?" Reaper asked.

"What's the big deal?"

This time King laughed. "Most of the women who encounter Payne find him scary as fuck. You walked right up to hug your friend. Never seen a woman do that shit."

Clara shrugged. "It has been too long since I saw Vicky. Now, I'd love a drink." She stretched her hands above her head, working out the kinks.

She made her way toward the stairwell, and she heard the men follow her downstairs. The club wasn't so bad. She'd seen far worse, and as she took a seat at the bar, Clara thought about staying in town for a little longer. She really did miss Vicky, and it had been too long since she'd had a good time.

The Soldiers of Wrath: Grit Chapter, looked like they could be rather enjoyable, and right now, she could do with some easy laughter.

Chapter Two

"Girl, I am so happy you're here," Vicky yelled over the blare of music.

Clara smiled and nodded. She leaned in, her beer in hand, the buzz moving through her pretty fiercely. "I know—me too. It's been too long since we saw each other."

Vicky smiled. "Let's not let so much time pass, okay?"

Clara nodded.

"Shot!" Vicky hollered out to the biker working behind the bar. He had tattoos lining his forearms, and she could even see ink coming up from the collar of his shirt and covering his neck.

He set a bottle of whiskey in front of them and two shot glasses. It had been a while since Clara drank, but tonight she was going to party. The people in the club seemed as if they liked a good time, and that's what Clara wanted tonight. She wanted to let loose, to just enjoy herself. She'd been traveling the country for the last few years, living off the money her parents had set aside for her, and the money she'd saved up over the years. Clara probably should have used it for college, but she figured she only lived once.

Vicky handed her the filled shot glass, lifted hers up, and together clinked the glasses.

"To having a killer fucking time," Vicky shouted, and Clara grinned.

She felt comfortable at the club, and how insane was that given the fact she'd just come here a couple of hours ago? She tossed back the shot, breathing through the burn of the liquor, and felt this tingling sensation on the back of her neck. Looking over her shoulder, she saw the biker named King staring at her, his focus intense, dark … promising. Everything in Clara tightened, and she blindly reached for the bottle of alcohol, needing another shot. She couldn't deny she hadn't felt this electricity move through her when she first saw him. He was a huge man, tall and muscular, sporting tattoos over his arms and probably on every square inch of his body.

"Looks like King has his eyes set on you, girl," Vicky said, and Clara turned and looked at her friend. "Oh yeah," Vicky said as if she saw Clara's confusion. "You better watch out, because when King wants something, he goes after it until it's his."

Clara finished her second shot and stared at her friend. "Did he go after you?"

Vicky shook her head. "Nope. I've been fucking Payne for a while now and when Payne has pussy on the mind, he sticks to one woman. For a while, at least."

Was King the same way? The truth was Clara didn't need anything more than a good time and wasn't that why she'd come back to Grit? She knew hanging with Vicky would ensure that, but could she let her inhibitions go and let her arousal lead the way? Hell, it might be fun just to think outside of the box and have a one-night stand.

"Hey, baby." The club whore came up to King, smiling, looking drunker than hell and smelling of sex. She reached out for him, stroking his leather cut.

"Get the fuck off of me," King said and pushed away the drunken club bitch who was moving her hand down to his cock. He looked at Clara, the woman here to party with her friend Vicky, and looking fucking good as hell. He glanced down at her ass, the jeans tight as hell and showing the big roundness of the globes. Damn, he'd like to slide his dick right between the cheeks, fuck her good and hard, and have her come undone from it.

"Want a hit, man?" Smalls asked, walking up to King and handing him the roach.

He took the roach, inhaled from it while he watched Clara take some shots with a few of the Patches and club whores, and felt his cock jerk at the sight.

"She's fucking hot," Smalls said and took a seat. The club whore moved away from King and went to Smalls, and thank fuck for that because he wasn't in the mood for her.

He looked at Smalls, knowing he had a grim expression.

"What?" Smalls asked.

"Stay away from her. I'm calling dibs." Yeah, he'd just gone there. He didn't want any of his fellow Patches getting in on her. King leaned back in the chair, the shadows in the corner hiding him slightly but giving him a prime shot of Clara.

"She doesn't look special to me," the club whore said.

He couldn't help but grunt. "She isn't dirty; that's for fucking sure."

"Hey, I like dirty," Smalls said and grinned over at the club whore. He pulled her onto his lap, grabbing one of her tits.

King went back to checking out Clara. She was dancing with Vicky, and it was clear she had a wild side. He liked that. God, her ass was full and round, her hips flaring out and giving him a prime shot of the fact she was all curves. The sweet butts at the club were thinner with bones protruding. But Clara had it going on, with thick thighs and a rounded belly that was shown whenever she'd lift her arms. He was getting so damn hard right now. King didn't give a shit who saw him take her.

"Come on, King. I'm right here, ready to give you whatever. Hell, I'll give it to you and Smalls at the same time if you want." She tried to grab for his cock again.

"I said not interested. Smalls, take the bitch and go fuck her or something." The Patch grinned and held onto her. Smalls pulled her shirt down, exposed her big, but clearly fake tits, and started licking at them. King turned his focus away from that scene and looked at Clara again, vowing to make her his, even if for only one night.

Chapter Three

The shots had given her one hell of a buzz, and any worries she did have started to fade away. Clara tipped another shot back and moaned as it burned her throat.

"So, what have you been up to?" Vicky asked, taking her own shot.

"Not a lot. Been on the road, doing some travelling. I've worked at a couple of places as a waitress, nothing permanent." She shrugged. It had been a fun couple of months, taking long walks down the beach, staying in a rented apartment, and working in her spare time. Clara didn't want to be tied down to a mortgage, and so it worked for her to rent. It was dead money but she only lived once.

"Any guys?"

She shook her head. "Not really. There was one guy who had a thing about sniffing my feet. I have to say, it was totally weird."

Vicky spat her mouthful of beer, covering the bar as she did so. "What?"

"Liam was his name. He was a server at the restaurant where I worked. He was hot, and so damn nice. Neither of us was looking for anything serious. Anyway, to cut a long story short, after he'd given me an orgasm, which was substandard at best, he pulled out of me, tore the condom off, grabbed my feet, and started to sniff and lick them while he jerked off. Let's just say, once he was done, I was out of there. Seriously, not my fetish at all." She shuddered, recalling how weird it had suddenly gotten.

Vicky burst out laughing and started to snort as she did.

"How are these men?" Clara asked, asking about the bikers.

"None of them have feet fetishes. Not that I know." She started chuckling. "They've all got a bit of kink to them, but it's more hardcore. But they're good guys, too. So far, Beast is the only one taken. He's with Bridget, and get this shit, she's his step-sister."

"Really?" Step-siblings getting together wasn't a big deal to Clara, although it was a little surprising. They weren't related—what was the big deal?

"Come on, let's go and dance." Clara was pulled off the barstool and dragged to the center of the dance floor. Several people were already on the floor, naked and dancing. Vicky threw her hands in the air and started to sway her hips. Clara did the same, and the music seemed to get louder. She gave herself over to the pleasure of the music, swinging her hips.

Vicky grabbed her hand, and they danced close, their breasts touching as they rubbed against each other.

"Girl on girl action drives them crazy," Vicky said, whispering the words against her ear.

"Do you have a thing for that guy who you were sleeping with?"

"Yeah and no. It would be cool to become his old lady, but I doubt he'd make someone like me his."

"What do you mean? He likes fucking you. Do you get along?"

"Yeah, we do. There's just rules here. A club whore is rarely an old lady." Vicky shrugged. "I don't think I'm anything special."

Clara stared into her friend's eyes and saw that she wasn't lying. They had always been different in high school together, neither of them wanted dates or to have long-term boyfriends.

"You are special, and don't you forget it," Clara said.

Vicky chuckled, spinning her around and then resting a hand on her stomach. Clara stared across the room at King, Payne, and Smalls. They all sat around a table. King had his focus on her, and she found it hard to look away.

"King wants you," Vicky said.

"You've said that." Clara continued to look at King, feeling a shiver move through her.

"I wonder how far we can go to tempt him?"

"You think I want him?" she asked.

"Honey, King is worth the effort," Vicky said. "Do you want me to stop?" She nibbled her ear, stroking fingers up her body, rubbing along her nipple.

"No, don't stop." Although girl on girl never really did anything for Clara, she couldn't say they hadn't fooled around with each other back in the day. Vicky was her closet friend, and they'd shared everything together, done everything.

Opening her eyes, she looked at King again and then at Payne. She saw the fire in both men's eyes, and she had to wonder how this would all play out.

"Fuck me," Reaper said, taking a seat beside Smalls.

King didn't take his gaze away as Vicky stroked her hand up Clara's body, cupping her breast. His cock threatened to punch a hole through his jeans. He wanted inside her, and by the end of the night, she was going to be bouncing on his cock.

"Fuck yourself," Smalls said. "Are you done with Vicky?"

"No. Touch her and I'll shoot your balls off," Payne said.

"Well, this show is for you two," Reaper said.

"How do you figure?" Smalls asked.

"King's staked his claim, and Payne's not going to give Vicky up. I guess I'll find another willing pussy who'll do some girl on girl action. That shit is fucking hot." Reaper moaned his appreciation and then got to his feet. "Good luck."

Smalls cursed and stormed off.

"Then there were two."

King took a sip of his beer. "Do you know anything about her?"

"Not much. She's the one friend who has been there most for Vicky. They talk on the phone, and I gather they are really damn close." Payne leaned back, clearly enjoying the show.

Clara spun around and locked their fingers together. King's cock thickened even harder. He wasn't going to be able to take much more.

"Are you thinking what I'm thinking?" Payne asked.

"Going onto that floor, taking the woman we want, and go into a private room?" King said.

"Fuck yeah. You want to come in and watch?" Payne asked.

"Why not? Both of them look pretty into it," King said, finishing his beer. He'd been too long without a good fuck. There was something about Clara, he didn't know what, but he wanted to fuck her. He wanted to know if she was going to be as hot as he imagined or if it was all just made up in his mind.

"That's what I'm talking about." Payne followed behind him.

Vicky and Clara were still dancing close when he wrapped an arm around the woman he'd be claiming tonight. Payne took Vicky.

"What do you say we take this somewhere private?" King asked, biting her ear.

Clara sighed and spun around. She looked a little shocked at first, maybe because he was being so forward, but she wouldn't have danced like that for them if she didn't want some dick.

"I want you." He saw her swallow.

"Do you have condoms?"

"Yep."

"Do you have some lube?" she asked.

King smiled. Yeah, he was going to enjoy this woman.

"Yes."

"Then lead the way."

Chapter Four

God, she was really doing this. Clara could blame the alcohol she'd drank at the bar, but the truth was from the moment she'd seen King watching her, clearly wanting her, she'd been all about him. She might not be as wild as Vicky, but Clara had done her fair share of being wild, and it looked like this experience was going to get crossed off her bucket list.

Sleep with a rough biker in front of Vicky, who in turn got fucked. And neither of them giving a shit about anything but this one moment.

She followed King, Payne, and Vicky into this back room, and once the door was shut she was surprised how quickly everything went down. Payne had Vicky pressed up against the wall, his hand shoved up her skirt, and was thrusting against her, all seemingly at the same time.

Before she could really take this all in, King had her in almost the same position as her friend. He had his lower half pressed to hers, his cock big, long, and very hard.

"Tell me you want me, baby," he said in a harsh voice. "Tell me you want my big cock."

God, this man liked to talk dirty, and fucking hell did she like it too.

Maybe she should have played hard to get, but the truth was Clara was ready to live on the edge tonight. She was ready to just forget about everything.

"Tell me what you want," he said again, grinding himself harder into her.

"I want you." She didn't know what had gotten into her, but she didn't want to stop. He leaned down and nuzzled her at the same time he ground his cock into her. In the next second he had his hand on her bottoms, had them undone, and pushed them down her thighs She kicked them aside, her panties the only thing now covering her pussy. He started grinding into her again while making harsh sounds, erotic and sexual ones that made her wetter.

The base of his shaft pressed into her clit, sending sparks of electricity through her. "Christ, baby, you have no idea how good that feels." He pressed more firmly against her, and her mouth opened on a silent cry. Clara was feeling pleasure she'd never thought possible.

King kept hold of her with one strong hand on her waist and used the other to reach between their bodies and rub her pussy, focusing on her clit.

She turned her head and saw Payne and Vicky were already fucking, her best friend moving up and down on the wall as she held onto Payne. The other biker was going crazy, pounding into her, making high-pitched cries leave her friend, and causing even more arousal to fill Clara. She wasn't getting turned on because of what was happening with the other two people in the room, but more so that the entire space was charged with electricity and chemistry.

"Does it turn you on watching them, knowing they are just a few feet away?"

She found herself nodding to what King said.

"You just want me to fuck you, or you want me to tease you more?"

"Fuck me." She felt feverish, like she was about to explode if she wasn't doing this.

"But maybe I just want to make you suffer, have you begging me to let you come."

She shook her head, seeing the grin on King's face.

"Nah, my dick's about to explode as it is. I want that sweet pussy already." He grinned wider. "I can have my wait with you another time."

Another time? No, Clara wasn't going to be some biker's pussy on demand. Hell no. This moment was about her and getting off, just forgetting about everything and anything and living in the moment.

Clara wasn't a virgin, but she also hadn't been with a man that was so well-endowed, and even if she hadn't seen what King was working with just yet, she could feel his size through their clothing.

And then King took a step back, unzipped and unbuttoned his pants, and pulled his dick free from the fly. She felt her eyes widen at the size, knowing he'd been big, but not realizing he'd been *that* well-endowed.

"No time for a bed," he grunted out, still stroking himself. "Take the fucking panties off."

She did as he said faster than she thought was even possible. Underneath the length of his cock was pierced, and she felt her heart race.

He's sporting a Jacob's Ladder.

He donned a condom and was right back in front of her, had his hands on her ass, and lifted her off the ground. She wrapped her legs around his waist, felt his cock probe her pussy, and knew this would be painful but also so damn good.

"Put me in you," he grunted out.

This might be a quick, one-night stand fuck, but it would also be so fucking hot.

"Yes, God, yes, Payne," Vicky screamed out, clearly coming.

He closed his eyes, clenched his jaw, and said, "Put my dick in your cunt."

She reached between them, grabbed his huge length, and felt the barbells under his dick. She moved the tip up and down her slit, and then aligned it at her pussy entrance.

"Yeah, this is going to be so damn hot." And then he pushed the tip into her. "Fuck," he grunted. "You're so tight and wet."

Clara closed her eyes at the delicious way he stretched her and at the feeling of his piercings hidden only by a thin layer of latex moving against her sensitive flesh. "God." She felt delirious for this.

The burning pain and ecstasy slammed into her as he continued to push all of those long, thick inches inside of her. But soon that discomfort left her as the pleasure increased. He moved his hands behind her and gripped her ass in a bruising hold.

"You're so fucking tight and hot. I love this, love your pussy snug around my cock." His voice was guttural, and his eyes were closed. She had never felt this way before, had never even thought sex could feel this good. Looking at Payne and Vicky still, she saw her friend was looking at her over her shoulder. Their gazes locked, and she wondered how deeply she actually felt for Payne.

"Does it feel good, baby?" King asked in a harsh voice, pulling her away from her thoughts.

"Yes. God, it feels so good."

With one more thrust he buried the last inch of his cock into her and groaned deeply. They both let out a hard grunt of pleasure, and Clara curled her nails into his back, loving how he filled and stretched every single part of her. She glanced at her friend, seeing only the way Payne's muscled back was in her view and how Vicky's legs were wrapped around the biker's waist.

King pulled out and then pushed back in just as slowly. His breath became quicker when he started thrusting in and out of her, and the heavy sac beneath his dick slapped against her ass.

"Oh my God." She felt her eyes widen, knew her orgasm was imminent, and tightened her hold on him.

"That's it." He groaned. "Dig your nails into me. Make it fucking hurt, baby."

It was agony and ecstasy all rolled into one. With every thrust of his hips she moved up on the wall, and she fucking loved it. A high-pitched gasped left her. "More. God, *more*." Here she was, begging him for it harder and faster. He never stopped his steady thrusting. He lowered his head, and his mouth was right by her ear. She tightened her hold on him.

"Fuck yeah." His voice was a rough whisper. The root of his cock rubbed along her clit, back and forth, again and again until that burst of pleasure escalated.

Her entire body tightened, signaling her climax. The pleasure rushed to the surface and stole all of her sanity. "I'm close, King." His name came out of her on a gasp.

"Come all over my cock, baby." He thrust hard and severely into her, hitting something deep that had her inner muscles clenching around him violently. "Yeah, that's fucking it."

Clara arched her neck and opened her mouth on a silent cry. Her climax took everything out of her, stole her energy, her strength, and replaced it with this euphoric sensation. He slammed into her, pressing his body fully against hers now as he continued to pump his hips back and forth.

Her thighs ached from how wide they were spread, and her skin was slick with perspiration. King bottomed out in her, almost slipped free from her body, but then just as quickly slammed back into her.

The sounds that filed the room were raw, exploding with sexual chemistry, and Clara was right in the center. She felt as if she'd just fallen off the face of the world and she didn't care where she landed.

But she knew, just knew, King wasn't nearly done with her yet.

Chapter Five

King took the joint from Payne as the two women snuggled up together. The way they behaved, it was like they didn't care that two men laid on either side of them, butt ass naked, and who they had both fucked. The women he'd been with who played with each other, they did it all for show and when the action was finished, they left. There was no lingering, no talking.

Taking a long pull on the joint, he stared down at Clara. Her pussy had been so tight, the tightest one he'd been inside in a long time.

"I can't believe you're here," Vicky said.

"It was time to move on. You know me—I can't settle down." Clara had her hands fisted together and resting underneath her chin. The only sign from her that she had been fucked moments before were the slight bruising on her hips. After they had fucked against the wall, he'd finally taken her to bed, and the two women had been talking nonstop.

"You're staying, right? Usually you come in and out of my life so damn fast, and it has been months since I last saw you. Please, please," Vicky said.

"You can stay here if you want," Payne said, which surprised the shit out of King. No woman was allowed to stay at the clubhouse unless they were giving their pussy, mouth, or ass for service. Staring at Payne and Vicky, he saw how his Prez always seemed to be touching her, stroking her. What the fuck was going on there?

He'd known that Payne had sort of staked a claim on Vicky, but it wasn't old lady kind of ownership.

"I'm not going to be fucking men while I'm here. I like sex, but I won't be used," Clara said. She looked at her friend. "No offense, Vicky."

"None taken. It's a lot different than you would think."

"I'm just not interested in being passed around."

"She's not," Payne said. "You can stay here, and you'll be protected. I'll put the word out."

"You'd do that for me?" Vicky asked.

"Yeah, I would."

A look was shared between the two, and King had to wonder about their relationship. He couldn't recall the last time he'd seen Vicky with someone else. None of the guys had been bothering her, and they looked toward her, but they never actually touched.

"I'm going to head to the kitchen, grab us some snacks. You girls stay here," Payne said.

King climbed off the bed, tugging on his jeans as he did. He followed his Prez out of the room. The party was still in full swing, and once they closed the door, Payne flicked the key in the lock, keeping the women safe.

"What's going on with you and Vicky?" King asked, walking in the direction of the kitchen.

"Nothing."

"I'm not stupid. Something is going on." They entered the kitchen and went straight for the fridge. "You've not claimed Vicky."

"And I'm not going to. Everyone knows not to touch her."

"Why haven't you claimed her?" King asked. He didn't get it. If Payne had feelings for Vicky, which he clearly did, why didn't he claim that shit?

If the women found out, they could make it a hard time for Vicky, which in turn could send her away.

"Look around you, King. This is no place to be claiming a woman."

"Beast did it."

"Well, Beast isn't the one that shit falls on, is it? It's me. I'm not going to put any kind of woman in that position, not even Vicky."

"You're protecting her?"

"I'm trying to. It's not always easy, but I'm trying to."

"If you claim her as your old lady, we'd all make sure nothing happened to her. You don't have to be living in fear of shit like that."

Payne shook his head. "It's not up for discussion."

"What are you going to do when she gets tired of being pushed away? A woman like Vicky, she's only going to be pushed so much."

Vicky was a fiery woman, but she was also a gentle one, and in time, she'd no longer see Payne as a man to love but a man to hate.

"I'm not letting her go. No matter what happens, she belongs to me, and she's going to stay with me."

There was no way Payne and Vicky were going to last. The explosion was going to rock both of their worlds. When it happened, King hoped there was a way to keep the club whole.

"What is going on with you and the badass biker?" Clara asked, declining the smoke that Vicky offered her.

"I don't know."

"Something is going on. I've never seen you look at a man the way you look at Payne."

Vicky smiled, blowing out a puff of smoke. The scent of the weed actually made Clara feel sick, but she wasn't about to make her friend quit it.

"I'm in love with him."

"Does he return your feelings?" Clara asked.

"I don't know. He rarely talks about his own feelings. The club, it has to come first."

"And you come second or last?"

The smile on Vicky's face disappeared. "It's not like that, Clara. The club, the MC, it can be dangerous, scary so, and when you're posed with the prospect of death, you don't play by the rules anymore."

"Vicky, I don't like you being here."

"You've been here a couple of hours. You don't know the guys, and you don't know how much I love it here, and I do. Please, give it a chance."

"If he hurts you, I'm going to kick his ass. I mean it. I'm not having you hurt," Clara said when her friend just kept on smiling.

"Clara, I've missed you." Vicky wrapped her arm around her neck.

She didn't care about their nakedness. It wouldn't be the first time they had shared a bed, naked, and been this close. They were the best of friends, and nothing was ever going to take that away from them. "I mean it. No one hurts you."

"Fine, I completely agree, but now you've got to promise to do something for me?" Vicky asked.

"Sure, anything."

"Well, it's two things."

"Tell me what they are, and I'll try."

"First, you've got to stay and give Grit a chance."

"Ugh, how long?"

"At least two weeks. It has been so long that you've got to promise I'll see you for the next two."

"Okay. I can handle two weeks. I'll find a job."

"Payne will have something for you to do."

"Providing it doesn't involve me using my body for board."

"He won't do that. He's not a very, erm, he's not a very hard— Look, he's fair, okay? Besides, let's change the subject. What do you think of King?"

Clara felt her pussy twinge at the reminder of King. His dick was so damn big, and he'd taken her to heaven and back. It had been too long since she'd had an orgasm, and especially one that made her tingle from head to toe. Even now the memory of his cock made her want to have sex even more.

"I see that face, you dirty little whore," Vicky said, laughing. "I was so damn surprised you just let loose and went for it."

"Don't even start." She smiled. "I honestly can't believe I did what I did either. It was like another person in me just took control. He knows how to handle himself, I'll give him that." Clara's cheeks heated even though she had nothing to be embarrassed about.

"One time certainly won't be enough."

"Stop trying to meddle," Clara said, closing her eyes.

The door opened, and she remained still as both men came in. The door closed, and the bed dipped. She opened her eyes in time to see Payne taking a kiss from Vicky. "We brought snacks," King said, showing off a bag of potato chips.

Her stomach chose that moment to growl.

"Here, enjoy."

Sitting up, she tore into the potato chips and started to eat.

"So, Clara, are you staying or are you going?" Payne asked.

"I've agreed to two weeks—"

"She needs a job," Vicky said.

"I can find my own job."

"She thinks you're going to make her screw or take her clothes off."

Clara rolled her eyes. King wrapped an arm around her waist, cupping her hip, and leaned into her. "You don't need to worry about work."

"I don't."

"There's always something to do around the club, and it's not just about sex. We can find something."

"I want the money so I can move on," Clara said.

"Move on?"

"I've only agreed to two weeks. When those two weeks are over, I'm going to move on."

"You never settle down?" King asked.

"There's no point in settling down in one place. I'm young. Life is meant to be lived and enjoyed."

"And you don't think it's capable of being done in one place."

"I know it's not. Life gets boring and predictable."

"She's been running from that all of her life," Vicky said.

Staring at her friend, Clara didn't have any witty retort or a comeback. She had no words.

Clara didn't believe that she had been running away from anything. She simply hated the sameness. Life was meant to be lived but if she settled down in one place, there was nothing to look forward to. That wasn't running away.

"Maybe you haven't found the right person to stay with," King said.

She turned toward the man who had been in her life for a matter of hours. He had a great cock, but other than that, she had no intention of anything developing between them. "It's not about finding the right person. Some people are made to stay in one place. I'm not made that way."

"You don't want a family?"

"No, I don't. I don't want to get pregnant, or get married, or settle down with the picket fence." Clara looked down at the potato chips, and any appetite or desire she had was now all but gone. It was once a dream of hers, but that had soon faded away. It was easier to be alone than to commit to someone. "You know what? It's getting late, and I think it's time I checked into a hotel room."

Chapter Six

You need to make up your damn mind.

Clara lay on the motel bed, staring at the stained ceiling, wondering what in the hell was wrong with her. She'd been at the clubhouse for only a few hours, fucked some random biker, watched her friend get screwed as well, and then she'd bolted out of there.

Scrubbing a hand over her face, she exhaled, knowing these next two weeks would be hard. It wasn't because she was staying here and not wandering like she had been doing, but because she knew she'd be seeing king again. There was just something about the big biker that had every part of her tightening. Her frightened her, but not in the way that she feared he'd hurt her. He scared her in the way that told her he was dangerous, would kill with his bare hands, and didn't give a shit about the repercussions. He was the type of man that did what he wanted when he wanted and when he'd held her, touched her, everything else had faded away.

Clara had never been loose with her body, and although she'd been with men, enjoyed herself, she never felt anything toward them except that initial arousal, but with King the chemistry had been instant, and she'd been so swept up in it she hadn't known what to do aside from just react to it all.

Even now her pussy was still sore from King's big cock, and the remembrance of what they'd done played through her mind on repeat.

The truth was she'd never seen herself with a husband or family, but that didn't mean having it in her life wouldn't be nice to have. Clara had also explored things, just let the wind take her where she should go. Not having to worry about anything or anyone but herself let her fully experience life. Thinking about having a man by her side, someone strong and opinionated, someone who made her feel this tightness in her gut, this flutter in her heart, had heat filling her.

Be realistic. You think King wants anything to do with you aside from the easy piece of ass you gave him?

She closed her eyes, knowing that was the truth. She'd stay two weeks, enjoy her time with her friend, make a little money, and then she'd be off to explore more of the world. She didn't need anything more than what she enjoyed.

But even thinking that had her feeling a little detached.

King sat behind the desk in the meeting room and went over some paperwork, a half empty bottle of vodka on the table beside him. He hadn't bothered with a cup and shouldn't be thinking about anything aside the orders for the hardware store they'd dipped their fingers in.

Trying to clear his mind, he reached for the bottle and took a drink straight from it. The hardware store was a newer venture for the club, something that was legit, and a place to clean any dirty money they had rolling in. The original owner, Hank, was old and had been diagnosed with cancer. It was a shitty outcome, but they'd known the man for years. He'd helped them out many times, and getting into business with Hank would mean his business wouldn't go under. The club would make sure his legacy stayed alive, and they'd also have a good place to clean their money for the business.

But staring at the paperwork didn't help his concentration, because all he could think about was Clara. It had been less than twenty-four hours since they'd fucked, and although he'd been with plenty of women, had never had any attachment to them, there was something different about Clara. She made his stomach tighten, his heart beat a little faster, and the very thought of her being with any other motherfucker made him see red.

He grabbed a joint and brought it to his lips, lighting up the end and then inhaling deeply. Leaning back on the chair and staring at the wall across the room, he pictured her in his head. He'd gone with her and Vicky to the motel to drop her off. Vicky had complained, wanting her to stay at the clubhouse, but Clara was headstrong. He liked that about her, like a strong woman that knew what she wanted in life, and Clara definitely did.

He took another drink from the bottle, his body relaxed, but his need for her just as strong as it had been hours before. Thinking about going to that motel room and fucking her senseless played through his head, but for as much as he wanted her he wasn't about to rush her either, not in that way. He may not be in love with her, but he definitely felt something instant with her, something he'd never felt with any other woman before. There was something magnetic, electric with Clara, and fuck did it turn him on. He could see her not giving in easily, could see that resistance that made his cock hard. As it was the fucker was like a steel rod between his thighs, wanting to be buried in her tight, wet cunt.

Of course, keeping her at the clubhouse had its perks, and thinking about her in his bed for the next two weeks sounded like a good fucking idea, but she'd come to him on her own, just like she had tonight. He had patience, and he knew one thing without a doubt ... he wanted Clara for more than one night.

And when King wanted something he wasn't going to stop until it was his.

Chapter Seven

"You could come to the clubhouse," Vicky said.

"Not going to happen." Clara moved around the motel room, grabbing some of her makeup, and walking toward the mirror. She had only been in Grit for twenty-four hours, and surprisingly, and very gratefully, had been able to find a temporary position at a hardware store. The sweet old man, Hank, had given her a job on the spot, after she had answered only a few questions. It was really funny, to be honest. He would only hire her if she could point to different tools and give him a little clue as to what they used for.

The most obvious one, he asked her to find a hammer. Seriously? Did men here not know that women knew what a hammer was?

"You could work at the clubhouse."

"Look, Vicky," Clara said, moving to stand in front of her friend. She cupped Vicky's cheek and pressed a kiss to it. "This is *your* life, okay. This is not my life. You're a club woman, and you've got something going on with the Prez, and I respect that.

Please, respect my decision that I don't want to spend my two weeks inside a biker club."

"They'd leave you alone. I promised you, you wouldn't have to fuck anyone or anything, and I mean that."

"I missed you too," Clara said. She stepped away and finished brushing her hair before tying it up in a ponytail.

"Was this because of the sex? It has been a long time since we had sex with each other."

Clara held her hand up. "We didn't have sex with each other, okay. We had sex with other guys in the company of each other, and I don't mind." She really didn't. It was something they had actually done a lot when they were in high school. Mostly that had been making out, though.

"If you're working away from the club, I'm not going to see you."

"You're going to see me. You're here right now, and if you ever want to do any DIY, you know where to find me." Clara gave her a wink and chuckled. She grabbed her purse and walked toward the door. "Are you going to see me out?"

She didn't have far to walk. Clara had gotten the motel within the center of the town of Grit. The hardware store was about a ten-minute walk along one stretch of road with shops on either side. She rather liked the quaint little town. Only there was nothing quaint about the bad-ass biker club that ruled the town.

Vicky pouted, and Clara kept on chuckling. "You've not seen me for months, honey, and now you're pouting."

"All those months you weren't here for me to talk to, and now you're here but you're going to be busy."

"I like working. You know that."

"I also know it's going to be the key to making you leave. I don't want you to leave."

"You don't?"

Clara closed and locked her motel room door. Wrapping an arm around her friend, she pressed a kiss to her head once again.

"You're my sister in the only way that matters, Clara."

Releasing her friend, they both started walking in the direction of the hardware store. "I'm not leaving for two weeks."

"You see, that's my point. You're going to leave. Is settling down really all that bad?"

"Vicky?"

"Please. I know you, and I know with this job you're going to get bored and when you're bored, you're going to move on."

They had both stopped in the street.

"I'm not like you." Clara forced a smile. "Can we stop making this complicated and just enjoy the fact, we're here, we're together?"

Her friend finally nodded. Vicky was always dependent on her. Clara wondered if her friend would have found herself in a biker club if she'd stayed. Pushing those doubts aside, she hugged her friend. "I'll stay for as long as I can."

"I'll see you later today? Lunch?"

"Sure."

Clara waited until Vicky walked away before making her way toward the hardware store. Hiking her bag up her shoulder, she made her way through the open front doors,

Hank was at the front desk of the hardware store as she entered.

"You made it."

"I did. Am I dressed appropriately?" She wore some jeans and one of the company shirts with the logo on it. Giving him a little twirl, she smiled.

"Damn, the guys are going to be coming in by the thousands to get a look at you."

"You're a charmer, Hank."

"I tell you, if I was twenty years younger."

He gave her that look that let Clara know he wasn't thinking very appropriately. Hank was a sweetie. He had a couple of daughters himself, and she'd seen the way he was with the ladies, never crossing that line.

"Only twenty?" she asked, raising a brow.

Hank gave her a wink.

"You're a horn dog. I'm going to go and put my bag in the back. Okay?"

"Sure thing. I'll just open up the store." She started toward the staffroom, when Hank called back to her. "The guys who have taken over the store will be stopping by to look over the books."

"I thought you owned this place."

"Oh I do. I can still work here, and I don't have to worry about all the other shit. I'm just here until the good man takes me."

Clara frowned, staring at Hank. She didn't know that anything was wrong with him. "Is everything okay?"

"All up here is okay. It's the damn body. Cancer—it's a bitch, right?"

"Cancer?" Clara didn't like that.

"Don't think about it. Go on, I'm going to open up, and I already see the parking lot filling up."

Gritting her teeth, Clara entered the staffroom. After placing her bag in the locker that Hank gave her, she slammed it closed and rested her head on her arms.

Cancer had a lot to answer to. She'd worked as a care worker in a hospital children's ward. God, that had been the worst few months of her life. She had been around sick kids, loving them, coming to see how strong they were, and then losing them.

"Ah, fresh meat," a guy said, entering the staffroom.

Clara took a deep breath, stepping away from the locker room.

"Bill?" she asked, seeing the other employee Hank had told her about.

"That's right."

"Nice to meet you."

Heading out to the store, she went toward Hank, who was waiting for her. For the first hour of the store opening, Hank shadowed her while Bill did the work. There was also a Ben, Tiffany, and Lance who worked at the hardware store. All of them seemed friendly enough. It didn't take Clara long to get into the swing of things. When she wasn't serving, she was helping people find what they were looking for. Of course, most of them knew where everything was. Several of the men who visited tried to get her to go out with them. Of course, that was not something she ever did.

"Oh wow, it really is happening," Bill said, looking over her shoulder.

Clara held a box of cables, and she looked behind her to see several of the Soldiers of Wrath: Grit Chapter members heading into the store.

"I want to prospect with them. They're so fucking bad ass. You've got to prove yourself that it makes college hazing seem like child's play," Bill said.

She recognized Payne and of course King. Her pussy went wet instantly at the sight of him and the thought of what they'd done. She hated the reaction she was having. Would she ever be the same?

Chapter Eight

King wasn't going to lie and say he was at the hardware store because he needed some fucking tools. No, Vicky had come back to the club looking all sad and shit, and he'd overheard her talking to Payne. She was upset Clara wasn't hanging at the club and when she mentioned she'd gotten a temporary job at Hank's, well, King knew what he wanted to do.

Ever since he'd been balls-deep in her tight little pussy she'd all he'd been able to think about. Fuck, he hadn't even been able to get hard for any of the bitches at the club, not that he wanted to. But before Clara came into the picture he'd had no problem getting wood just watching some pussy rubbing up and down on the stripper pole at the club. No, he shook his head, now all he saw was Clara.

Maybe he just needed another piece of ass? But he wanted more than just that sweet ass, wanted more than her tight fucking cunt riding up and down on his cock.

He heard the little bell above the door at Hank's hardware go off, but his focus was on Clara. She was behind the counter, her eyes wide as she took note of him. It was clear she was right in this moment as he was, and that felt pretty damn good.

"I bet she's wet right now," Payne said from beside him, and King turned and clocked him in the arm.

"Watch it, man," King said, his focus already back on Clara. She had her head turned away, and he could see her cheeks were red. Fuck, he wanted her again. His cock was already semi-hard just from the thought of bending her over the counter and fucking her so hard she couldn't walk straight after the fact.

"You got it bad, King," Payne said again, but he moved out of the way just as King was about to deck him. Payne started laughing and walked to the cordless tool section. "If you're going after that piece then go after it already. I got shit to do at the clubhouse."

King ignored Payne and walked up to where Clara stood. There was a guy close to her, staring at him and his cut.

"H-hey, man," the guy said, slightly stuttering the words out. King tipped his chin but didn't respond. He just looked at Clara again.

"You're avoiding me and the club, why?" Although he'd heard enough from Vicky talking, King wanted to hear it from Clara. She looked at him then, her eyes slightly narrowed. Oh he liked the fire in her. Turned him the hell on.

"I don't need to explain anything. I'm not going to be here for very long anyway."

He cocked an eyebrow and leaned against the counter, his arms crossed now. "So you just wanted my cock and now you're tossing me aside?" He could have laughed at his statement, but he kept his expression stoic.

She snorted and looked at the other man, who didn't even seem to be listening to their conversation.

"Like you've never fucked a woman and tossed her aside."

He shrugged. "Never said I didn't do that. I asked if that's why you let me be balls deep inside of you. You just itching for some dick?" He watched her cheeks get pink again, and he grinned.

She glanced at the other man again. "Can you give us a minutes, please?"

"Leave," was all King said. The guy scurried off, and King turned back to stare at Clara. "You wanted him gone because I embarrassed you?" She didn't answer, but she didn't need to, because the way she acted was proof enough.

He'd gotten under her skin.

"Yeah, you embarrassed me because you talked so bluntly about what we did."

"You don't strike me as the type of woman that gives a shit what people think."

She narrowed her eyes. "I don't care, but you and I don't know each other all that well, and I don't want my business spread out all like that."

He grinned wider.

She huffed and crossed her arms over her chest, causing her breasts to plump out even more.

Damn, I want her in my bed, under me, and butt naked for me to worship.

"You think this is funny?" she said, but he could see she was fighting a smile.

"I do." He leaned forward on the counter, loving that she didn't back down. "And I think you're thinking this is a good time, too."

She rolled her eyes, but smiled. "Listen, I'm going to be upfront."

He grinned and nodded. "That's all I'd expect from a person."

"Look, why is everyone giving me a hard time about making Grit a temporary stop?" She shrugged. "You've known me for a day and Vicky and I could carry on a friendship if I were on the moon." A moment of silence passed. "But if you're looking for something more," she shook her head, "I can't give you that."

He cocked another brow. He wasn't about to admit that was exactly what he wanted ... more. He could let her think what she wanted, that he'd be okay with her lying down with him, but the fact remained he wanted a hell of a lot more with Clara. He often didn't run across things he couldn't figure out, but with Clara he was finding she was one of those things that had him up in knots. He wanted—no—needed to lean more about her.

Clara sagged when King and Payne left the store. She'd actually gone there with him, despite telling herself she wasn't going to. This was not what this trip was supposed to be about, but here she was in this "temporary" job, agreeing to have some kind of sex fling with a biker.

If I'm going to be here, I might as well enjoy myself, right?

"God," she whispered. This was bad, because she felt something for King after that one encounter. It wasn't love but was obviously lust. It wasn't just that, though. There was chemistry, an electrical charge between them she'd never felt before.

This is either going to fuck everything up, or be one of the craziest rides of my life.

Hell, she would bet money that this experience would be both of those things.

Chapter Nine

At the end of the day, King was waiting for her. He stared at the front entrance of Hank's store, watching her and Hank through the front window as she closed things down for the evening. Hank was a good guy, and he was pleased that the older man had decided to give her a chance. It had been so long since she'd been to Grit that she was like a new person. In Grit the locals at times were very pessimistic about outsiders, especially ones that are just passing through. At least she didn't have to worry about that.

Grit had a lot of bad history with shit like that.

The Soldiers had to leave their little clubhouse to come and take care of things—deal with shit. The locals, of course, rarely ever said thank you, maybe too afraid deep down. But the MC didn't give a fuck. There had been several petitions over the years to try to ride them out of town. Nothing had stuck, and nothing was ever going to stick either. They brought too much money into this town and allowed a lot of people a way to earn a living.

If the club was to move, pack up all of its shit along with all of its legal businesses, then Grit would fold within a month and turn into one of those ghost towns.

King was across the street, partially hidden by the shadows. He watched as Clara left the shop, walking beside Hank.

She stopped, laughing at something the man said and clutching her stomach at the joke Hank had clearly told her. Knowing the old boy, it was something dirty.

He smiled. Clara was a good woman. He liked her, and even though he didn't really know her, from what he'd heard Vicky say, Clara would be the kind of wife who'd love her husband completely.

Why did she feel the need to always be on the move?

Clara was a good woman, a strong woman. She'd make a perfect old lady. She was a force to be reckoned with.

They moved closer to him, and Hank stopped and grinned at him.

"I see your boy is here," Hank said to Clara but stared at King. "Be warned, King. If I was twenty years younger, I'd be the one taking this lady home."

Clara chuckled.

"Make it thirty, old man. Don't even try to lie about your age. We all know you're old."

"Ah, the cocky little shit is trying to show you he's big and bad, Clara. Don't believe him."

"I don't." Clara was smiling. "I've come to see men like to talk a big game. They all act the big bad but when you kick them in the balls, they all crumble at your feet." She gave Hank a sweet smile. "So, we're closed on Sundays, but we open bright and early Monday?"

"You're going to be here come Monday?" Hank asked.

"I don't know. Probably. I promised Vicky I'd stay for a while, and I hate to let her down."

"I need to send Vicky something. She's helped out at the shop a few times without wanting to be paid."

"Don't worry," Clara said. "She's just as happy with a box of condoms."

They all laughed.

"Right, I'm going to leave you young kids in peace."

King and Clara watched as Hank drove out of the parking lot. "I like him," Clara said. "He's a sweet guy."

He wasn't about to be the one to tell her that he was dying.

She came across as being this strong, independent woman, but he couldn't help but wonder what pain she was hiding. Clara was a woman hiding from something, he just didn't know what.

"He does okay. He's happy with the club, and we've saved him a time or two in the past. Some bastards tried to rob him. Instead of calling the cops, he called us, and we were here and took care of the little shits." Yes, he was bragging. For some reason he wanted to look good for Clara. He wanted her to see him as a man that could protect her.

"Good. I'm glad. So, what are you doing here?"

"I was thinking you could come for a ride with me."

"Really?"

"Yep."

"To the clubhouse for sex?"

King gave her a wink. "I like your thoughts and if that's what you want I'm game, but I was thinking just a ride first," King said. "Climb on." He handed her an extra helmet.

"This better be worth it," she teased.

"Trust me. I'll make it more than good for you." He watched as she put her backpack on, placed the helmet securely on her head, and then climbed on the back of his bike, wrapping her arms around his waist.

"Okay, hot shot, what now?"

"Now, you hold onto me, and I show you how good this can be."

He pressed on the gas, drawing up his clutch, and they jerked forward. Clara gave a little squeal, holding him a little tighter. "Don't forget to hold onto me, baby."

"Asshole. You did that on purpose."

King wanted her holding onto him a little tighter, squeezing him.

His cock was already rock hard. The woman had been working all day, and her scent was driving him wild. What the fuck was wrong with him? She still smelled fucking sweet.

This time when he started to drive his bike, he did it slowly, and they rode around the parking lot. Clara chuckled.

"You've made your point. Ride a little faster, buddy. I want to know you mean it."

"Do you mean the bike or my dick? I'm happy to use both."

"Show me what you can do on the bike, and we'll get to your dick later." She reached down, taking hold of his cock. "What's the matter, baby? Can't think?"

He groaned, but he took her on a ride. She was one hell of a little minx, that was for fucking sure.

Gathering speed, he pulled out of the parking lot and rode along the main road. She didn't let go of his dick, rubbing him through the fabric of his jeans. When they were out of the main town of Grit, he picked up his pace.

Clara had no choice but to hold onto his waist. "This is it, King."

He wished he could see her.

Instead, he had to be happy with her excited squeals instead.

For twenty minutes he rode fast, making her scream, gripping his waist as she held him tighter.

Finally, he pulled into a spot near the mall where a lot of teenagers usually went to fuck around. Yeah, he never said he was a gentleman or that he wanted privacy. He just wanted seclusion, and this place offered it for the most part.

Turning off his bike, he waited for her to climb off, and then he was there. Grabbing her arms, he pushed her back until she hit the wall. No one would see or hear them, but he wouldn't have cared either way. King new this place better than anyone. From the moment he was part of the Soldiers, he'd made sure to know everything, and everyone. It was why he was giving the part of being VP.

Claiming her lips, he plunged his tongue into her mouth as she moaned.

"King," she said, the sound muffled by his kiss.

"You've been fucking torturing me, and now you're going to reward me."

He slid his hand inside her jeans, finding her soaked panties. This woman was a fucking dream. There was no way he was ever going to let her go.

No fucking way.

Chapter Ten

A gasp left Clara when King latched his mouth onto hers.

His kiss was hard, demanding. It was exactly like the man King was. He tilted her head, controlling her so that she was helpless against him, that he was the one kissing her like he owned her. King was every kind of bad for her, but at this moment, at this exact time, all she could think about was how his mouth on hers was doing wicked things to her body.

The cold, rough surface of the brick wall met her back as he pressed his chest against hers, sandwiching her between him and the building. His hands slid down her hips and around so he was cupping her ass. He gripped the edge of her shirt and slowly dragged it up until it was bunched under her breasts. He then pushed her pants and panties down. He dropped down to his haunches so that his warm breath blew across her bare folds, and all Clara could do was groan in pleasure. Maybe she should have stopped this, but she couldn't help herself when she was with King.

"Spread for me, baby." She did as he said and then he gripped the back of her knee and brought it over his shoulder. His mouth was suddenly on her cleft, his tongue parting her folds as he ate her out. Knowing that anyone could see them at any given time was surprisingly erotic and turned her on even more. With his hand on her ass, he started to squeeze the flesh at the same time his tongue dipped into her opening. It hurt slightly but also felt so damn good.

He fucked her with his tongue and it took everything inside of her to hold herself up. The rough scrape of the brick on her back added a hint of pain to the unbelievable ecstasy he was bringing her. The hand that had been gripping the back of her knee snaked between her thighs and as soon as his thumb touched her clit, she came.

A low, keening cry left her and she speared her hands in his hair and shamelessly ground her pussy into his face.

Damn, he knows how to work it.

The grip she had on his hair was hard and she knew it had to hurt him, but his groan told her he liked it. He gave her pussy one last long lick before standing. She saw the glossiness on his mouth, and knew that it was his pussy cream that had made it like that.

He kept his hands on her ass and pulled her forward, letting her feel the hard length of his erection against her belly. He pressed his lips against hers, ran his tongue along the seam before plunging into her mouth. She tasted herself on him, and it turned her on even more. She wrapped her arms around his neck, but he stepped back almost right away.

"I want you on your knees, hands behind your back." His command was rough and held no room for argument.

Clara swallowed, feeling her pulse increase and her pussy become so damn wet. It was like she hadn't just had an intense orgasm. Her pussy clenched for something substantial, for something that only King could give her.

"Just do what I say, Clara."

The way he was exerting his dominance, as if he just expected her to submit, was so damn arousing she couldn't help but give him what he wanted.

She dropped to her knees and felt the hard, gravel-laden ground dig into the flesh of her knees. The thick jut of his cock was right in her face and she looked up at him.

"Give me your hands, baby."

She brought her hands behind her back and clasped her fingers together, doing what he commanded. She wanted to do whatever he said. The way he looked down at her, how he ran his fingers along the edge of her face, tracing her cheekbones, her chin, had her feeling as if she was the only woman in the world for him, or, at least, this one moment in time. Hell, they'd been around each other for such a short time, but it had been the most intense experience she'd felt thus far. In all her travels she'd never wanted a man like she did King. He was wrong for her, so very wrong, but a part of her wanted it badly.

He took himself in hand and brought the head to her mouth, teasing her, making her hungry for him. The tip brushed against her lips and she immediately opened her mouth. She used her tongue to tease his cock head and licked up the thick vein that ran on the underside of his shaft. He groaned his praise, told her how good she felt, what a good girl she was, and that made her hotter, wetter. Clara started moving her head up and down, doing exactly what he liked, what he ordered from her, because she wanted his cum in her mouth. She wanted to swallow it, to taste it filling her mouth. He may have her on her knees, submitting before him, but at this moment, she held the power.

Chapter Eleven

King stared down at Clara as she bobbed her head on his cock. She tightened her lips around his shaft and then glided her lips down as far as she could go. He loved the feel of the tip of his dick meeting the back of her throat. Each time she took him into her mouth, the farther down she went.

"You're like a little fucking dream, aren't you?" he asked.

What was it about this woman that drove him wild? He didn't even know her, not really. She was just some woman, and the club was full of different kinds of women. He loved fucking them, and with the club, he was always guaranteed variety but easy pussy. That's what he loved, easy pussy. Clara wasn't necessarily easy. She didn't spread her legs for any dick that swung her way. King probably shouldn't be pleased about that, but he was. He'd fucked plenty of pussy during his time—none of them were worth settling down for.

Settling down?

"Do you love sucking cock?" he asked.

She moaned, shaking her head at the same time.

Pulling out of her mouth, he watched as she licked the tip.

"I think you're lying."

"I don't like sucking cock."

"You were going at mine like a starving woman."

"I know. Isn't that strange, considering I don't like doing it, but with you, it's so fucking hot." She sat back on her knees. The gravel digging into her knees, and he couldn't wait another second.

Gripping her arms, he eased her up and sank his fingers into her hair. She tasted so damn good.

"Um, you still have the taste of my pussy on your lips," she said.

Pressing her back up against the wall, he spread her legs. Her jeans were already gone, so it was easy to get her into position.

"You like a little bit of pain, a little bit of danger, don't you, baby?"

"You're about to fuck me out in the open, what do you think?"

He loved her sassy mouth. Tilting her head back, he claimed her lips, sliding his tongue into her mouth. His cock pressed against her ass but at that moment, he was more interested in her lush lips. They were so thick and beautiful. Her lips looked amazing wrapped around his cock.

"You're so fucking beautiful," he said, whispering the words against her lips.

"Fuck me, King."

Gripping his cock, he found her wet entrance and started to slowly sink in deep into her pussy.

They groaned together as he filled her tight little hole.

"Feels so good," she said, moaning.

"That's right, baby, so fucking good."

"Wait, you didn't put on a condom."

He growled. "Fuck, I'll pull out."

"What the hell? You know you can still get pregnant like that."

"I thought you were safe."

"I am safe. Fuck, it doesn't matter."

He silenced all of her protests by slamming his cock deep within her pussy. She cried out. Grabbing her hands, he pressed them above her head and started to fuck her. Only their hands were pressed against the wall—he held her away from the rough brick. He liked his sex hard and rough but he wasn't going to hurt her.

"You're so fucking wet. You can't go anywhere. I'm addicted to your pussy."

She gasped and chuckled. "I doubt I'm the first woman to hold your interest with this."

Biting onto her neck, he flicked his tongue over her rapid pulse. "I've had a lot of pussy, and none of them have been as tight and as wet as yours." He pulled out, glancing down to see her cream glistening on his naked shaft. "I've never fucked another woman without a rubber on. I take care of that shit."

"Shut up and fuck me."

He silenced her again with the pounding of his cock. King was starting to figure this woman out. She loved to be in control, she didn't like to be controlled, but also, she was afraid of connecting.

King wasn't going to give her the chance to run away.

"Vicky says you get bored real easily."

"You're going to talk about Vicky now?"

"We were in the same room when she was screaming like a banshee riding the Prez's cock."

"That's different."

"No, it's not."

Pulling her hands above her head, he reached between them to finger her swollen clit. The instant he touched her nub, her pussy tightened around his cock, making it impossible for him to pull away from her. He wanted answers, and he wanted to bargain with her.

Clara had a history of just getting up and leaving. Vicky told him that she sometimes got informed when Clara was on the road, but rarely did her friend say goodbye.

"She doesn't do goodbyes. She says that saying goodbye means she's not coming back, and she has every intention of coming back."

He'd seen the pain in her eyes. She loved her friend, and it hurt her every time Clara disappeared.

"I want you to stay."

"What is it with everyone begging me to stay?"

King slammed his dick back inside, watching the pleasure cross her face. He was going to get his answers one way or the other, and if making her wait for release got him what he wanted, he was going to do it. "What is it with you fighting it?"

"You can't force me to stay in Grit."

"I know I can't force you. It doesn't mean I can't try and persuade you." He paused with his dick deep inside her. This was the better time than any to have this conversation. She was distracted, pinned, and he could get what he wanted from her.

Chapter Twelve

Clara didn't want to talk about leaving, not at a time like this. Truth was she wanted to settle down, had even thought of staying in Grit and seeing where this went with King. But she was afraid. She'd been traveling the country her whole adult life, and finally calling a place home again seemed a little weird. It also didn't help that she didn't know King all that well aside from them having sex, but their connection was undeniable.

"You're making this worse." She hadn't meant to say anything out loud but as soon as the words left her, King stopped and pulled back enough that he could see her.

"I'm making this worse because you don't want to stay, or you want to so fucking badly it scares you?"

She felt her mouth part but didn't know how to respond.

"I know you feel this with me, too." He started thrusting slow and easy inside of her. "I know you want to see where this goes, but you're fucking scared."

"I don't want to do this right now." And she didn't. This was getting too deep. "I just want you to fuck me, King."

"You want me to stop talking about it?"

She nodded, but she knew it wasn't believable.

"I'll stop for right now, but this isn't fucking over." He stared right in her eyes. "You want me to fuck you until you don't have to worry about anything else?"

She nodded, needing it.

"Fine, then you got it, baby." He started thrusting in and out of her hard and fast, and she moaned.

He fucked deeply, never stopping, never relenting. Instead he latched his mouth onto her breast and sucked her nipple until her clit pulsed and more wetness spilled from her. Over and over he tormented her until the pain and pleasure morphed into one and she wasn't just thinking of begging him—she actually was.

"Yes," she moaned. "Fuck me."

He was pressed fully against her, gripped the cheeks of her ass, and held her like she weighed nothing at all.

Mouth parting on its own when she felt his length slip through her slit, Clara wrapped her arms around his neck, pressed her breasts against the hardness of his chest, and was now the one kissing him brutally. It was like a floodgate was opened and all of her passion, desire, and need for King came bursting through. Clara had to stop the kiss and gasp at the feel of being stretched so fully by him. Big, long, and thick were all perfect words to describe King and when he started thrusting in powerful strokes, she knew she would come within minutes.

"Christ, baby." King panted against the side of her neck and never stopped pumping in and out of her. "Yeah. That's it. Milk my cock. Get all the fucking cum out." He grunted and groaned against her. Their flesh was already becoming slick with their combined perspiration, and she held onto his shoulders tighter as he became frantic in his motions. "You feel so fucking good." He scraped his teeth along her neck, and a shiver worked its way through her whole body before taking root in her clit.

"God, yes, King." Every time he thrust into her the base of his erection rubbed the hard bundle of nerves and had her silently crying out.

"So good, baby. You're so fucking tight and hot, and so damn wet for me." He took control of her mouth with his once more, but this time it was a sloppy, heated, and almost angry kiss.

She tugged at his hair, loved the dampness at his scalp because he was fucking her so hard. The gritty brick abraded her back as she was moved up and then slid back down on it with every violently delicious thrust. Even though they'd already fucked, this experience was so damn erotic. Neither of them could control themselves, and as their bodies grew wetter from sweat and their touches became painfully good, she knew she'd come harder than she ever had.

She had to be hurting him by digging her nails into his back, but all he did was grunt against her mouth, tighten his hold on her ass, and fuck her harder.

He pulled back only long enough to look at her chest. "You have the biggest, most mouthwatering tits I have ever seen." He still had his hands on her ass and when he spread the cheeks, slipped his fingers between them and touched her anus, everything inside of her tightened. "That's it, come, Clara, because I want to see you so fucking unhinged you can't even see straight, baby."

And just as she was coming he said, "But we aren't fucking done with the conversation, Clara."

She felt her eyes widening as her pleasure soared. "I want you as mine, and that means you'll have to stay in Grit."

Chapter Thirteen

"You finally made it back," Payne said.

King looked back at his Prez and shrugged. It was the following morning, and he'd spent the entire night with Clara. They'd gone back to her hotel room, and he'd fucked her to the point her neighbor in the next room had complained.

"I didn't realize you were keeping track of me."

"I wasn't. Your lack of presence was noted. Even Beast saw, and he's always inside his pussy these days." Payne was smoking a joint, blowing out a puff of smoke.

"Where's Vicky?"

"She's sleeping. You don't need to worry about her."

"I'm not worried about her."

"Vicky's worried you're going to break Clara's heart."

"So now you're being a pussy and going to ask me not to hurt your girlfriend's friend?" King folded his arms, staring back at Payne. "You won't even declare Vicky as your old lady."

"What I feel for Vicky and how I treat her is not your problem. Vicky becomes upset, so do I. I don't like that."

King snorted. "Seriously, when are you going to accept that you fucking love that girl? From the first day she got here, you couldn't stand for another guy to touch her, and yet you let them until you had the balls to actually do it yourself."

Payne stood up, taking several steps toward him. "You better watch your fucking mouth."

King wasn't about to stand there and take a warning from his Prez, when the only person really hurting Vicky stood right in front of him.

"What's the matter, Payne? Don't you think that you not taking her as your old lady is going to hurt her? You treat her like this fucking treasure that no other brother can touch, and yet, you won't even give her the chance to be your old lady."

"You know why the fuck that is."

"Because of some enemy? Yeah, you're more scared of some fucking enemy that's not even come out yet. You're my Prez and my friend, but don't think for one second that I'll let you tell me what to do when it comes to the woman I'm fucking. If you do, this will go both ways, and I'll let Clara right at your ass."

"Don't fight," Vicky said, startling both of them.

Payne took a step back, and King glanced toward the door. She wore one of Payne's shirts, and it stopped at her knees.

He also noticed the pain and the hurt in Vicky's eyes.

"What's the matter, baby?" Payne asked.

"I heard you shouting, and I was worried."

"You've got nothing to be worried about. We're all fine down here."

"Did you just get in, King?" she asked.

"Yeah. I spent the night with Clara."

"How is she?"

"She's fine. It's not easy to figure out what she's thinking."

"No, it's not."

"Why don't you go back to bed, babe," Payne said.

"It's morning. I don't want to."

Vicky moved into the room, going toward the coffee pot.

"What's Clara's story?" King asked.

He figured she'd be the best person to know what he was up against.

"You expect me to spill all of Clara's secrets?"

"You're best friends with her. You're going to know a lot more than me, and the best way of actually keeping her here in Grit."

Vicky sighed, and her shoulders drooped. She turned around, nursing her coffee. "You'd think I'd know how to keep my best friend in place, but the truth is, I don't know how."

Payne moved up beside Vicky, and King was shocked when she stepped away from him. Usually Vicky was the one vying for Payne's attention.

"Why does she move around a lot?"

"Most of the time Clara gets bored with where she's staying. She'll move on to try to find something exciting, something different. When that doesn't happen, she tends to always find a reason." Vicky chuckled. "You know, when we were in high school, she was the one who wanted to have the family, the kids, and settle down. That's not the woman she is now though. Over time she changed, and it stopped being what she wanted. Now, you can't keep her in one place."

The woman who wanted to settle down was not the woman King knew—far from it.

"What made her move away?"

Vicky shook her head. "No, I can't do it. Clara's my best friend. If she wants to tell you why she travels, then it's up to her." She turned to look at Payne. "You don't need to go warning him about what it would do. Regardless of who forces Clara away, her leaving will hurt."

"Baby," Payne said.

"No, I can't do this right now. You're not fair. I promised you I wouldn't do this in front of the club, and I won't." She glanced toward King, and she gave him a smile. "I'm going to get dressed."

She left the room, carrying her coffee along with her.

"Fuck!" Payne ran fingers through his hair, looking pissed off.

"If you ask me, Prez, the only person hurting that girl is you." King slapped him on the back.

"She knows why I can't claim her."

King was tired of hearing the same old excuses. It pissed him off. Yes, there were dangers out there, but if the club knew she was Payne's old lady, she'd be more protected than club pussy. Their enemies were many, and they didn't care who they killed to hurt the club. Club pussy was expendable to some of their enemies. The club did what they could to keep them safe, but there was only so much they could do.

"I'm going to catch a couple of hours."

Leaving his Prez, he made his way toward this room and found Vicky sitting on the steps, sipping at her hot coffee.

"What are you doing here?"

"Sitting, waiting."

"What are you waiting for?"

"You to go so I could talk with Payne."

"He does love you, you know."

"It's kind of hard to believe when he won't even accept me." She sighed. "Forgive me. I promised to never be that girl. The one who was waiting for the man to appear and sweep her off her feet. This is a fucking MC, so that's never going to happen."

"It doesn't mean you can't wait for it."

"I'm realistic, King. I love Payne with my whole heart. I'd risk everything for him. I'd die for him, but he won't even risk having me as his old lady." She patted his knee. "It's fine. I'm pleased you're not giving up on Clara."

"Would you like to talk about it?" he asked.

"Nah. I'm going to drink this and head out."

He nodded. "Don't give up on him."

As he walked away, he was sure he heard her whisper, "I already have."

Chapter Fourteen

Payne paced his room, the door already shut, his anger mounting. He was pissed at the conversation he'd had with King, annoyed the other man had all but called him out on Vicky. Payne cared about the woman, but fucking her and calling her his old lady were two totally different things. He scrubbed a hand over his hair.

"Fuck," he ground out, not having been this pissed in a long time, and it was because of how he felt for Vicky. But she was in the club, fucked him, and although she was exclusive to him, that didn't mean he had to make her anything but his fuck buddy.

The sound of someone knocking on his door had him glancing at it.

"Fuck off." He turned away, but there was another knock. He growled low in his throat, stormed over to the door, and opened it. "I said fuck off—" Vicky stood on the other side of the door, wearing only a robe and a pair of high heels. He knew she was naked under there, and despite his thoughts, his anger, he got rock hard.

"Busy?" she asked in a low voice. She seemed nervous, or disconnected. Hell, she looked a little sad too.

"No." Payne stepped aside, pushing away anything he felt but lust. Once she was in the room he shut the door and crossed his arms over his chest, checking out the plump ass he could see under her robe.

She turned and faced him, and they held each other's gazes for long seconds. And then she untied the knot at her side, pushed the robe off her body, and stood there naked and ready.

"I don't want to think about anything but your cock in my cunt."

His dick gave a jerk and he groaned. "I can make that happen."

He needed the distraction from his thoughts, and he was going to take out all his annoyance over what he felt and what King said about Vicky. But fuck, she'd take it all and beg for more.

Vicky didn't know why she was here. Well, she did—because she loved Payne, but she was just setting herself up for more heartbreak. She'd told King she'd given up on him, and although maybe she had given up on Payne and ever having anything other than sex with him, she was a glutton for punishment. She loved Payne too much to just walk away. He was her everything, whether she ever told him that or not.

But right now she wanted him. Her body was wet, ready, and she didn't want to pass up any opportunity to be with the man she loved. Call it desperate, low, pathetic, whatever. She didn't care.

"You're so fucking gorgeous."

He body shook with anticipation listening to his words, and pleasure mounted higher inside her.

"I'm feeling like some pain mixed with pleasure might loosen us up, baby. What do you say?" He lifted a dark eyebrow.

She nodded and licked her lips. She knew what he wanted, what he liked. "Anything you want, Sir."

He made a low sound in his throat.

She always felt this pleasure when it concerned Payne. Vicky knew that even if she had no future with him, she'd take whatever he gave her. Maybe she was twisted, sad, pathetic, or all of the above for allowing a man to have his way with her but not make her his. But fuck it all.

Tonight there would be spanking until bruises formed, her being tied up, and an array of other deliciously wicked things, and she anticipated it all. He'd make her cry with pain, but above all else, he'd make her feel good.

Like all the bikers in the Grit chapter, he was hardcore, and didn't fuck around when it came to protecting his club and those he cared about. She loved that quality in him. But she was just pussy on the side to him, and God did that hurt like hell. Vicky would be lying if she didn't admit she wanted to be able to look at him and know she was his old lady.

Stop thinking about it. It'll never happen.

Closing her eyes because she knew how foolish these thoughts were, she tried to focus on the right here and now.

I'm like an addict looking for my next fix, and Payne is my drug of choice.

"You want to do what I say, baby girl?"

She nodded, feeling her body heat.

"You want to submit to me tonight, get rough and dirty?"

She nodded once more.

Vicky would always submit to him, anytime, anyplace, and for any reason. She was just a woman in love and wanted to please the only man she'd ever been in love with.

You didn't give up, not when you want this too badly.

Her pussy was wet, her nipples tight and hard, and her heart was racing.

"Turn around for me and present yourself."

She did as he ordered and stared at the posts on each side of the bed, the ones that had restraints on them. Her palms became sweaty as she imagined all the things Payne would do to her ... all the things he'd help her forget. She imagined him bringing his hand, his belt, down on her ass, making her cry out and beg for more. A shiver worked through her at that thought, at that images, and the memories of what she'd experienced with him.

"Spread your legs and bend over. I want to see what I'll be fucking hardcore tonight."

She bent at the waist, spread her legs wide, and clenched her hands in the sheets, feeling higher than a fucking kite because of her arousal.

This wasn't just a game to her. And maybe one day Payne would see her as more than just a warm hole to stick his dick in, but until then she'd keep coming back for more. That's what happened when someone was in love, right?

Chapter Fifteen

One week later

"You're still here," Vicky said. They were eating at the local diner, and Clara looked over at her friend who looked happy.

"I'm still here, and I'm still working for Hank." She liked working for the old man. He was so much fun, and she loved hearing his tales of love and loss. Some of it was sad, but he tended to make it funny, and she couldn't help but laugh. "How are you?"

"I'm great. I'm having lunch with my best friend, she's still in Grit, and that makes me happy."

Taking a large bite of her hamburger, Clara stared at her friend. "How is Payne?"

She was silent for a second, somber. "He's good." Vicky was looking down at the table, clearly lost in her thoughts.

"Are you exclusive?" Clara asked.

Vicky looked at Clara then. "Are you still screwing King?"

Clara didn't miss how Vicky changed the subject. "Yeah. Don't even think of turning this on me."

"You could move into the clubhouse, you know."

"I don't want to do that." Clara shook her head after she spoke.

"The men will keep their hands to themselves. I promise King will make it known no one is to touch you."

Clara sighed. It was her turn to change the subject, because she didn't want to even go down the King path right now. "You just can't face it, can you?"

The smile on Vicky's face dropped. "Please don't, Clara. And now you're the one changing the subject."

She hated seeing her friend hurting. Payne was using Vicky for his own personal pleasure, and he clearly didn't see what it was doing to Vicky.

But isn't that what King's doing to you? Isn't that what you're doing to him?

She shook her head at her thoughts.

"So, I was thinking a girls' night out might be fun. What do you think?" Clara asked, not about to push Vicky on the subject.

"Just us girls?"

"Yep. No dick allowed. I asked Bridget as well. She's coming along. I was thinking some drinks, some dancing, and no, it's not at the clubhouse. No dicks, no nothing. Just us."

Vicky clapped her hands. "I like that. I miss hanging out and partying with you."

Seeing the smile back on her face, Clara was happy. "Me too." Grabbing the ketchup, she squirted a large amount on her burger.

"You know ketchup isn't good for you?"

"Neither is the burger but I'm living dangerously. What are you doing this afternoon?"

"I've got to organize the club's files. They're a mess, and Payne asked me to do it," Vicky said.

Clara gritted her teeth and bit her tongue to stop herself from commenting on the bastard who was using her friend.

"Sounds fun," Clara said sarcastically.

"Loads," Vicky replied just as sarcastically. "But it's easy, and I get to sit on my ass all day."

They finished up lunch without another hitch or a problem, and Clara left her friend to head back to the hardware store. She paused when she clocked sight of the motorcycles right out front. Clara recognized Payne's. The urge to trash his bike was strong, but she held back. She just cared about her friend and hating she was obviously in love and hurting.

"I'm the sensible one," she said to herself before heading inside.

Walking into the hardware store, she saw Bill was staring at three bikers wearing the Grit Chapter leather jackets.

Her pussy grew slick and her pulse started to pound when she caught sight of King. He didn't see her, and she was glad. She needed to keep her distance from that biker if she knew what was good for her. But the truth was he was like a drug she was addicted to. He was rough and tough, but he was also kind of charming in that biker, badass kind of way.

Putting her bag into the staffroom, she made her way outside to where Bill was standing. She fired up the till, ready for customers. At the same time, she started to unbox several items that they displayed around the counter, trying to keep herself busy and her sight and thoughts off King.

"Hey, Clara," Bill said.

"What's up?"

"Do you think I'd make it as a biker?"

She glanced over her shoulder, looking at the man. "Seriously?"

"They're so hardcore. It's what I want to be. I mean, look at those hotties over there. They've not been able to stop drooling since they walked in."

She rolled her eyes. "That's why you want to be part of the club? To get women?"

"It's not the only thing."

"I think there's a lot more than that to being in an MC." Bill shrugged.

"To be part of an MC you have to be loyal to them, Bill. It's their cause, and you've got to be willing to risk your life for them. It's not just about fucking your way around." *God, when the hell did I get so fluent in the whole biker world?*

There was a round of clapping behind her, and she looked over her shoulder to see King and Payne standing there staring at her. "I couldn't have said it better myself," Payne said.

Tucking her hair behind her ear, she felt her face heat at the praise. But she ignored them and finished doing her work. But she *felt* King's gaze, and she couldn't deny it made her pussy slick. The images of his wicked tongue between her thighs, showing her exactly how good it was to be naughty, nearly had her moaning out loud.

"You enjoy your lunch?" King asked, standing in front of her.

"Yeah, I did."

"Was Vicky with you?" Payne asked.

"Yes, she was." She didn't like Payne. Avoiding their gazes, she stepped behind the counter and started cleaning away. King reached out, holding her arm.

"What's the matter?" he asked.

She forced herself to look him in the eye. "Nothing."

"Something is clearly bothering you."

"Yeah, but it doesn't have to do with you."

Clara looked at Payne. He was wearing his leather cut, showing the whole world that he was a leader. She couldn't help but sneer at him. This man, he was hurting her friend, and he didn't even care enough to see it.

Vicky is a big girl, and this is her life and the way she wants to lead it.

"What the fuck was that all about?" Payne asked.

"Payne? What the fuck is going on between you two?" King asked, looking between them.

"No, King. She wants to give out dirty fucking stares, then let her. I'm not going to accept them unless she has a good enough reason."

Folding her arms, Clara rounded the counter and made sure nothing was between them. She wasn't afraid of this man, not when he was hurting Vicky's emotions. "Yeah, I've got a problem with you. You're a fucking asshole. What's worse, my friend doesn't see it. You're using her and getting what you want, but you're too much of a chicken shit to even see it yourself. You hide behind cowardly excuses, and that just makes me sick." Clara was not about to rein it in. "Can't you see what's right in front of you?"

"Don't for one second think you can come—"

Holding her hand up, she silenced him. She probably had a death wish, but she didn't care. "I've known Vicky my whole life, and she's in love with you, but she wants you so much she doesn't care what kind of relationship you're in. I know her, Payne. You're killing her with how you're using her."

"I'm not using her." Payne looked pissed. Good, because she was too.

"Then claim her as your old lady! You screw her and toss her aside. You don't see the real pain you're causing but it's going to get her killed."

"I would never let anything happen to her." Payne ran a hand over his hair, looking and sounding frustrated.

"Oh yeah, what about if it was to be at her own hand?" Clara let him think about that. "Vicky is a good woman, but she can only take so much. She has a history of ... hurting herself. If you keep pushing her away, if you keep on hurting her, and she doesn't see a way out, she gets down. I know Vicky. She's fragile when it comes to her love. Why do you think I try to see her often? You're the first person I've seen her really truly fall for, and that scares me. You put her at risk making her some club whore, but you don't even have the balls to claim her properly."

"She's a grown ass woman and knows what she wants," Payne growled out.

She pointed at King. "All of your boys, King included would protect her with their lives if you showed them that she meant something, but you just won't do it. Others may be afraid to stand up to you, but I'm not." She looked at Bill. "I wouldn't join the club—you're better than that." Shoving Payne hard, she walked away, not caring about the chaos she left behind.

Chapter Sixteen

Clara was sweating, but it was the good kind of perspiration, the kind that told her she was having a good time. The music was loud, pumping, and the club was packed with so many people she could smell the sweat and arousal fill the room.

Vicky and Bridget were dancing just a few feet from her, their smiles wide, and the obviousness of them having a good time made Clara feel good about making this night happen. She lifted her hand and gestured for something to drink, and Vicky nodded. Bridget did the same, and Clara pushed her way through the throng of bodies to go to the bar. The line was ridiculous, but she needed a little reprieve from the heat and suffocation of dancing in the club.

When her turn to order finally came up, she leaned on the bar and ordered three girlie but strong drinks. As she waited for the alcohol to be passed her way, she turned and faced the bar. She could see Vicky and Bridget still dancing, and she found herself smiling.

"Here you go."

She turned and faced the bartender. He wore a silver sequin top, his muscles pronounced, and the scent of his cologne washing through her.

Making her way through the throng of people once more, she handed the girls their drinks, and in record time they finished them, laughing. The buzz was strong within her, and although she was trying to keep her mind off King, it was hard as hell. This tingling covered her entire body and she glanced around the club, expecting someone to be looking at her. But all she saw was people dancing, sweaty bodies, and flashing, low lights.

"You only live once. Come on girls," Vicky yelled, and they started dancing again.

The music pulsated through her, and the heat and alcohol made her lightheaded. Clara closed her eyes, continued to dance, and got lost in the feelings of swaying, the heat in the room, and just feeling very good and content in where she was in her life right now. She didn't know how long she danced, but soon hands moving around her waist from behind her and warm breath along her neck had her tensing.

"You can move, baby."

Clara spun around and stared at the guy who stood behind her. The guy was clearly drunk and started swaying, his grin spread wide over his mouth. The scent of alcohol and cigarette smoke came off him strongly. He was also sweaty, the pit stains evident. She felt disgust that this guy had touched her.

"Fuck off."

He grinned wider.

"Hey, I can make that happen, baby." He wrapped his arm around her waist again, but Clara pushed him back.

"I said fuck off. That wasn't an invitation."

He stared at her, sweat sliding down his forehead, and then made a move at her again. He was either too drunk to realize what the hell he was doing, or he was a fucking idiot. Before he could touch her again she felt someone behind her, felt the heat as if it consumed every part of her. She looked over her shoulder, tilted her head back, and looked into the face of a very pissed off King. Payne and Beast were behind him, their expressions furious as well. Their focus was on Bridget and Vicky and when Clara looked at the other women, she noticed they were no longer dancing and their stares were locked on their men.

King's nostrils flared and his face was a mask of anger.

King pulled her behind him, and Payne and Beast went and wrapped their hands around the other two women's waists.

"King?" she said, but he either didn't hear her or he didn't care.

King was on the guy in a matter of a second. He slammed his fist into the side of the drunk's face, and the other man fell to the floor instantly.

"You motherfucker," King growled out, and the sea of bodies parted around them. He picked him off the ground and punched him in the face before letting him fall once more.

He went after the guy again, but she rushed forward and grabbed his shirt, pulling him back.

"He's not worth it. Come on, King." She tried to pull him backward, but it was like trying to move a tank. Clara sure as hell didn't want King doing this.

He stopped, looked over his shoulder at her, and the rage she saw on his face was like a blast of cold air. She let go of his shirt and felt her own anger rise. What in the hell was he even doing here?

"You think he shouldn't get the shit kicked out of him for touching you?"

She didn't say anything, didn't know what to say.

"I think we should go."

"No, Clara, He touched what wasn't his."

She lifted a brow. "I'm not yours, King."

He was silent for a second, his nostrils flaring. "Are you sure about that, baby?"

"God," she said through her anger. "What the hell? Why are you guys even here?"

"We're here to make sure you're okay."

She shook her head. "Girl's night out doesn't mean having bikers stalk us and lurk in the shadows."

King growled and stared at her as he wiped the blood off his knuckles and onto his pants. "You're mine, whether you want to fucking admit it or not."

God, seeing him wipe off the blood from the fight he'd just been in was hot as hell. Clara didn't respond, just turned and pushed her way past the crowd, and went outside. This had gone too far, but she didn't know if she was pissed about the whole thing, or if having King declare her as his was what she always wanted.

Chapter Seventeen

Clara looked so fucking sexy. King wanted to bend her over the nearest surface and pound the fucking shit out of her. Instead, he was pissed off and angry. What was it about this woman that was driving him crazy?

When they'd found out the women would be going to the club they'd been all for following them and making sure some motherfucker didn't mess with them. They could have stayed at the club, watched the pussy that hung out at the MC walk around and be flaunted in his face, but King wasn't interested in any of that. He just wanted one woman, and that was Clara.

Then he'd seen that punk ass drunk touching her, and sanity and civility had left him. He didn't want anyone touching what belonged to him, and whether Clara liked it or not, she belonged to him.

Watching her curvy ass walk away from him pissed him off, but it also turned him on.

King followed her outside and smirked when he saw how angry she was.

"What is your problem?" she asked, spinning around to face him.

"I don't have a problem." He crossed his arms over his chest and stared at her.

"You just went psycho on that guy for no reason."

He lifted a brow, his amusement fading. "No reason? Did you want his fucking hands all over you? He was drunk as a fucking skunk, Clara."

"You didn't have to do that, though. I was handling it. I could have handled it."

"You do that a lot, don't you, babe? You handle everything."

Clara folded her arms across her chest. "That is none of your business."

"Actually, when it comes to you, it is my business. My dick has been inside you, and you belong to me, so it is my business."

"And what in the hell are you doing here anyway? Did you three follow us?"

He didn't answer, and she looked as if she got even more pissed.

"I wasn't going to fuck him, King. This was supposed to be a girls' night out, and yet you three decided to come and what, rescue us if things got out of control?" She narrowed her eyes at him. "And you know I'm pissed at Payne. Why bring him along?"

"Payne and Vicky's problems are their own. Don't get involved in them," King said.

"She's my best friend. She's like a sister to me."

He stepped toward her. "Payne's not going to let you interfere with Vicky. You're lucky he let you get away earlier."

"He's an asshole."

King reached out, grabbing her arms. "Let it go, baby." He stared at her lips. "Is this what you do when you find someone you want, when you start to feel for them? Is this getting too deep, too heavy for you?"

She shook her head.

"You start to feel scared so you make sure it's someone else's fault for you to leave." He was starting to see through Clara's little act, and it pissed him off.

"You don't have a clue what you're talking about," Clara said.

"Yeah, I know exactly what I'm talking about." He took a step toward you. "Finding someone scares the shit out of you, doesn't it?"

She shook her head. "This is crazy," she whispered.

"It's not. You find a reason to leave every time someone gets close to you. What the fuck is it going to be, Clara? Are you going to run every chance someone gets fucking serious about you?"

Clara laughed. "We're not serious. You want me because I'm different from all that pussy at your club. Nothing is different here."

"Fuck you, Clara." He shook her, annoyed as hell with her. He was so damn mad. Payne wasn't mad at Clara but at himself for what he knew to be true.

"There's no one in this world that cares about me like Vicky does. That's why I don't want anyone messing with her or her emotions."

King shook his head. Payne wanted Vicky for more than club pussy—King knew that. Hell, everyone knew that, but Payne was too much of a stubborn hard ass to do anything about it.

"You need to just walk away from them and focus on us."

She pressed her lips together and he smirked. He was getting under her sin. "Come on, baby." He pulled her close and placed his hand between her thighs. "Let me fuck the stubbornness out of you—"

She brought her knee up, getting him in the balls hard enough that he went down.

He cupped himself. "Fuck!"

"You don't have any right to touch me like that, to just brush away how I feel." She was crying.

Staring up at her through the pain, King gritted his teeth. "I'm in love with you, Clara."

Silence fell on the whole of the parking lot, and she froze, her eyes widening. He heard the door of the bar opening and closing.

"What the hell?" Vicky said, shock in her voice.

Glancing behind him, he saw Payne, Vicky, Bridget, and Beast. Great, they were all about to see him getting shot down. And they all had probably heard what he'd said.

"Did you put him up to this because you want me to stay?" Clara asked, throwing the accusation toward Vicky.

"Of course not. I wouldn't ever do something like that."

Something was seriously wrong if Clara really believed that her own friend would get him to admit his feeling toward her. But she was crying heavily now, looking like she was on the verge of really losing it.

"Is it too hard for you to believe that others are capable of loving you?" Vicky asked.

"Don't," Clara said, her voice sounding tight with emotion.

"No. I'm not going to back down from this." Vicky moved to stand beside him. "What is *your* problem?"

"My problem? What about you? You fuck a guy who is using you. Before you start judging someone else, take a look at your own life." Clara was wiping the tears away as she spoke.

"This isn't good," Bridget said. "What are you doing, Clara?"

King saw the conflict in Clara's eyes. He didn't get it, nor did he understand it.

She shook her head. "No, I'm done. I'm gone." She spun around and started walking.

"Clara, no!" Vicky called out.

King saw the car coming toward Clara, but she clearly didn't notice it because her head was downcast. He ran toward her but didn't know if he was going to make it in time. He rushed as fast as he could, but the person driving clearly wasn't paying attention.

He watched as the car hit Clara.

Everything froze while his entire world crashed around him as he watched the woman he loved roll across the top of the hood of the car before falling to the asphalt.

King rushed to her side, wanting to pick her up but afraid in case he caused her any lasting damage. "Call a fucking ambulance," he roared out to whomever was listening. The car that hit her was parked to the side, and the guy that got out looked panic, afraid. King wanted to beat the shit out of the guy, but he stayed by Clara's side instead.

"Clara, Clara, oh God, I'm so sorry," Vicky said, now beside her. "That car hit her so hard. Is she breathing?"

He pressed his fingers against her neck, finding a faint pulse. "She's alive, but her pulse is faint."

"Ambulance is on the way," Payne said. "This is fucking crazy shit."

"Not now," King said. Clara had clearly been through a lot and obviously had a lot on her mind. It was clear she was afraid of commitment, but he couldn't let her go. "I love her, Payne. I'm not going to let her go."

"It's hard for her to let people in, to let love in," Vicky said and looked at King. "I think that's why she's so resistant to admitting she loves you."

"I'm not walking away from her. I promise you. I will be with her for the whole of my life."

He grabbed Clara's hand and pressed a kiss to her fingers. In the distance he heard the ambulance siren. Clara was going to make him fight to keep her, well, she had just met the stubbornest man in the Grit Chapter of Soldiers of Wrath. He was going to get her and keep her.

Chapter Eighteen

King was a fucking mess. He hadn't left Clara's side for the last two days, and although he wanted to scream at her to wake up, shake her to open her eyes, he was gentle with her, barely touching her for fear he'd hurt her further.

Vicky was sound asleep in Payne's arms in the corner of the hospital room. She'd refused to leave Clara, and he couldn't blame her, because he was the same way. He loved Clara, and her being hurt was eating him up alive. He wanted to just take her home ... to his home, to be the one to make sure she was on the mend. But the doctors had her in a sedative-induced coma to help lessen the swelling in her head. They'd started lowering the meds bit by bit to allow her to wake up on her own, but fuck, this was hell.

He leaned back in the uncomfortable as fuck chair, ran a hand through his hair, and breathed out. Even unconscious Clara looked so damn beautiful. All he could think about was their last conversation. What if she didn't wake up? What if he never got to see her beautiful eyes open again? What if he never got to tell her he loved her and hoped like hell she'd say it back?

Fuck.

He stood and started pacing, feeling like a caged animal.

"Why don't you go get some coffee, man?" Payne said, his voice thick with sleep.

King looked at the other man, knowing he was losing it but afraid to leave Clara.

"She'll be okay. We aren't going anywhere. Walk off the energy, King. You're strung tight and have barely left her side. You won't be any help to her when she wakes up if you're about to tear through your skin."

Aside from going to the bathroom and taking a five-minute shower in the bathroom attached to the room, King hadn't been away from Clara's side. This situation had made him realize he truly did love this woman, and he hoped like hell she came around so he could tell her that again.

The pain was the first thing she felt. It controlled her entire body ... her mind and very soul. But Clara couldn't move, didn't even want to for fear it would hurt too much. As she tried to think of what happened, the darkness took over, hiding what she wanted to know, what she needed to understand.

Her heart was racing, and she felt sweat line her forehead. Was it because she was in so much pain, or because she was scared as hell? Clara couldn't even catch her breath. Slowly opening her eyes, it took a second before her vision focused. At first she was staring at a white wall, but as she turned her head she realized she was in a hospital room. Shifting on the bed had her wincing and stilling instantly.

She lifted her arm to rub her eyes but realized she had an IV in the crook of it and a bandage wrapped around the entire length of her forearm. She could see a little bit of blood on the stark white bandage. Closing her eyes, she tried to think of what in the hell happened, and then like a flash of light behind her eyes, it rushed back to her.

The club.

The fight with King and Vicky.

The pain of getting hit by the car.

Groaning, she tried pushing herself up on the bed a bit more, and through the pain managed to prop herself up. Sitting in the corner was Vicky. She was curled up on a chair with a blanket wrapped around her. She rubbed her hand over her face but stilled when she felt another bandaged wrapped around her head. Sweat coated her skin, and she breathed out. Everything rushed through her mind, but it was still slightly hazy.

Her face throbbed and her ribs ached. After pushing away the blanket that covered her, she glanced down at herself. She was dressed in a hospital gown, and her leg was wrapped in a bandage as well. It hurt to even try to move it, so getting out of bed was a no-go. Scanning the rest of her body, she saw she was covered in bruises. Clara grabbed the edge of her gown and pulled it up as a tightening pain filled her. She had black and blue bruises that covered one whole side of her body.

Dropping the material back over her body, she looked around the room again. The door was shut, and the sound of the IV pump filled the small space. And then the sound of the door opening came through and King and Payne walked in. They spoke low and held cups. King was the first to see her awake and when Payne did as well, they both stopped. A moment of silence filled the room before King spoke.

"You're up." He was by her side a second later, having set the cup down to grab her hands. She stared at him, emotion rising up as she realized how close she'd come to dying. "You've been out for almost a week," King said, his voice tight. "After the first couple of days they took you off the meds you were in and out, hallucinating." He looked and sounded so damn happy right now.

Another second later and Vicky was on her other side, crying.

She looked between the two of them, the people she loved so damn much it hurt.

"I'm sorry," Clara wheezed out, her throat sore, her mouth dry. And then she started crying because the rush of emotions was too much to hold in.

Chapter Nineteen

"Don't cry. There's no need to cry," King said. The relief was instant at finally seeing her awake. He'd faced guns and a shit load of problems because of the club. None of that crap had scared him like this. The thought of losing Clara...he never wanted to go through that. Fuck, he loved her so much.

Other people had died from being hit by a car, and she'd looked so fragile and delicate that he'd only been able to see her gone from his life. He hated that. He hated being helpless while she was lying unconscious in a hospital bed. There was no one for him to fight to get his anger out. He could only watch and hope she pulled through.

"I'm so sorry. I was so stupid." She kept on sobbing, and he looked over at Vicky to see she was also a little startled by Clara's outburst, tears streaming down her cheeks as well. "I was such a horrible bitch to all of you, and I was so wrong."

"You need to calm down, Clara. You were hurt, and you also need to rest," Vicky said.

"I'm so scared."

King grabbed her hand. "What are you afraid of?"

"Being hurt, being left behind. The moment you start to love someone, it takes you, changes you and when you lose that person, you're never the same. I don't want to lose myself because I'm madly in love with you. I've lost people before. I can't handle losing anyone else."

She loved him. Clara fucking loved him.

"Oh Clara," Vicky said, tears spilling down her cheeks.

"I love you so much, King."

His heart swelled with the fact this woman was his, that she was willing to give him a chance. "I love you too, baby." Fuck, now he was getting all emotional.

"I love you, King. I don't know what you did, and I wish I could hate, because that would make things so much easier. But I can't. I love you so damn much, and it scares me. I'm not some young plaything. What if another woman comes along and excites you more than I do?"

He laughed and shook his head. Cupping her cheeks gently, mindful of her wounds, he smiled at the love of his fucking life. "You're a crazy woman if you think there is anyone else I could ever want. You're all I want, Clara. Do you think I'm not scared? I'm part of an MC. My life is not easy, and you deserve so much better than me, someone that isn't a criminal and a motherfucker." He leaned down to kiss her lips. "I fucking love you, and seeing you get hit by that car has put a lot of shit in perspective for me. I can't lose you."

"I love you," she said, again, crying and smiling at the same time.

"I love you too."

Pressing a kiss to her lips, King tried to be gentle.

"Okay, can we step back and give the doctor some room?" the nurse said from behind him, and he moved away, smiling at Clara.

Squeezing her hand, King smiled. "I'm just stepping out. We'll talk more as soon as the doctor leaves."

He stepped out, staring at her through the window as the doctor started to talk to her. His heart was racing. With how long it had taken her to wake up, he was starting to think she never would.

"I've never seen her cry like that," Vicky said. "It was kind of scary." She gave a little chuckle. "She's awake, and she's not going anywhere."

"Do you really think I'd have let her leave?" King asked.

"She can be stubborn."

"Babe, you've not been paying attention to King. He's worse than stubborn. He can be a big old pain in the ass," Payne said.

She chuckled, and he glanced back to see her resting a head on Payne's chest. "Thank you for staying with me."

"Always, Vicky," Payne said.

Staring back in the room, King looked at Clara as she nodded and talked with the doctor. Minutes passed, and he was finally able to go in.

Taking a seat on the bed, he took her hand once again.

"So I hurt myself, broke my leg in two places, my arm is broken, and I left some skin on the tarmac. Oh I also have a concussion. All in all, I'm peachy." She looked worried. "I have no insurance—"

"Don't worry about the medical bills. We can handle them."

"I don't want to do that."

"Babe, you're my old lady." *Fuck that sounds and feels incredible.* "It doesn't matter anymore what you want or don't want. It's what you're going to get. You're mine."

"Wow, you're very bossy," she said, but she was smiling broadly. "Note to self, human versus car, car wins, hands down."

Vicky chuckled. "We're going to get some coffee and give you time to talk."

Clara nodded, smiling. "I'm sorry—"

"Stop with all the sorry comments, babe. You're alive, and you love me. Life is good."

King laughed as Clara glared. "Fine, I'm not saying sorry to you again."

"You just did." Vicky winked, and he watched the couple leave.

"They're getting along better," Clara said.

"Vicky's stronger than you give her credit for."

"Yeah. I came to Grit to get myself together, and if anything, I've just made life hard. I'm not normally like this."

"What? Running away?"

"Talking about my feelings, getting to like a guy to the point that I want to stay. What did you do to me, King?"

"I made you fall in love with me, and you know what, over the years I'm going to make you hate me, make you wonder why the hell you stayed, but late at night when I'm deep inside you, or holding you, you're going to know it's because I love you more than any man could ever love you."

Tears filled her eyes, and her lip quivered. "God, what is happening to me?"

"I think deep down in that heart of yours that you tried to turn to ice, is a very sweet, very loving woman, who is afraid. You don't have to be afraid with me, Clara. Now, you're going to be coming home soon, and I'm going to be the one to take care of you. I don't want to hear any complaints from you. You'll do as you're told. Otherwise when you're well, I will put you over my knee and spank you for all those wrongdoings. Now, is that understood?"

"Yes, King."

Chapter Twenty

One month later

It had been four weeks since Clara was released from the hospital, and she still had this damn cast on her leg. She'd just gotten the cast on her arm taken off, as her fracture had healed nicely. But she hated that she couldn't do the things she normally did and was reliant on others to help her.

Looking out the window she saw King and Payne outside working on their Harleys. She'd moved in with King when she'd left the hospital. At first she thought it would be temporary, because truth was she liked being on her own. But being with King in the same house, having him take care of her, and him basically saying she wasn't leaving, felt really good.

It was a nice spring day, the sun was shining, and she was happy—like really happy. She supposed she could have had some drama in her life with an ex, maybe even a crazy stalker. But the truth was she'd been so reluctant about letting herself love King because she was afraid. Yeah, that was the big climax of the story of her life. She was weak and scared, afraid of being in love and giving herself to him, but then shit going downhill and her losing him. That was why she lived the way she did, was a rolling stone, and just lived life to the fullest. If she didn't settle down and let herself be happy and in love, she wouldn't be hurt. It seemed at the time like the safe and smart route to take, but the truth was she'd been lonely, so damn lonely.

Being with King these last few weeks had been the happiest Clara had ever been. She'd always thought she would love traveling, being alone, and changing her life at the drop of a pin. But she realized how much she'd been missing since being in Grit with King.

God, I love that man so damn much.

"You doing okay?"

The sound of Vicky behind her had Clara turning. She nodded. She smiled at her friend. The woman that had been with her through thick and thin. They'd been through so much in this life, but it was only the beginning.

"I'm good. Just thinking."

Vicky looked past Clara out the window, and Clara saw the pain flash across her best friend's face. During the last four weeks something had shifted, changed between Vicky and Payne, and not in a good way. But when Clara had first asked her friend about what was wrong, Vicky had closed up pretty tight. Whatever was happening between her and Payne was deep, and Clara understood that if Vicky wanted to talk about it, she would confide. Until then Clara would give her friend some space.

"You know I'm here for you," Clara said and moved over to Vicky. Well, she hobbled on the crutches.

Vicky nodded but didn't say anything as she started making sandwiches. "I'm probably going to head out after this. I have some things to do."

Clara knew what that meant: she didn't want to spend time here since Payne was hanging out.

"I can make Payne leave, Vicky. You don't have to leave because of him."

Vicky shook her head. "Thanks, but I really do have some things to do."

Clara stared at her friend, wondering what was going through her head right now.

Another twenty minutes and Vicky was saying goodbye. Clara stared out the window and watched her friend leave. Vicky kept her head lowered, purposefully not looking at the guys, and Clara's heart hurt for her friend. She wished she knew what in the hell she was going through so she could help her. But, if this life taught her anything, it was she needed to step back and let people live their own lives the way they wanted. If Vicky wanted to talk, she knew Clara would be here. She'd always be here.

Vicky's heart was thundering, her palms were sweating, and she was scared as hell.

She looked down at her hands and twisted her fingers together in her lap. What in the hell was she going to do if this was really her fate? Shifting on the table she sat on, the paper gown she had on crinkled.

What in the hell am I going to do?

There was a knock on the door a second before it was opened.

"Vicky?" the woman in the white lab coat said. She looked down at a file and then glanced at Vicky again, smiling.

"Yes," Vicky said, her throat tight, her mouth dry.

"How are you doing?" the doctor asked.

Vicky shrugged, thought about lying, but figured she'd just be honest. "I'm scared as hell."

The doctor gave her a sympathetic smile. "That's normal." She set the file down and pulled over a machine that had been pushed against the wall. "So you're here for verification?"

Vicky nodded. "Yes. I took three tests at home but wanted to make sure."

The doctor nodded and started working on the machine. Vicky stared at the screen that was currently black.

"Go ahead and lie fully back. The test we ran came back positive, but because you've said you have a history of miscarriages?" The doctor glanced at her, and Vicky nodded.

"Just one, when I was in high school. I was very early along."

"We'll just make sure things are okay, so we'll do an internal exam."

For the next few moments Vicky watched the doctor get the machine ready, and once the internal exam was underway she felt her heart seize as she saw that black screen light up.

The doctor turned the screen more toward Vicky and smiled. "There's your baby. You're about five weeks' gestation."

Vicky couldn't speak, couldn't even think as she looked at that little bean-shaped thing on the screen. That was her baby, hers and Payne's baby.

God, how in the hell was she going to get through this alone? She sure as hell wasn't going to bring this up to him, not since he'd completely shut her out for unknown reasons over the last few weeks.

No, Vicky was doing this alone, but she knew she could do it. She could handle anything.

I hope.

Epilogue

"What are you doing?" Clara asked.

"Well, we can't have sex yet, but I think you need some light relief." King spread her thighs open, and she gasped as his tongue found her pussy. "So sweet and so tasty."

"Why are you torturing me?" she asked, gasping as he flicked his tongue across her clit.

She loved his touch, and since getting out of the hospital, King had kept his distance. He'd been driving her insane with need, and now she couldn't handle anymore.

"Fly to Vegas with me," he said.

"Um, why?"

"To get married."

"Can't you wait?" She cried out as he thrust two fingers inside her. "Oh God, you're not playing fair."

"You promised to be my wife, but you won't just fly out and marry me."

"Damn you!"

"Agree, or else I will spend the rest of the day torturing you until you do."

He sucked her clit into his mouth, and she couldn't believe that he was using oral as a way to make her agree to fly to Vegas.

She tried to thrust her pelvis up to make him give her an orgasm. He held her hip in one hand, while with his other, he fucked his fingers inside her.

"Come on, baby, come for me, if you can."

"You bastard!"

She couldn't fight this. There was no way she could hold out.

"Yes, I'll go to Vegas with you. I promise."

King made her come, and she screamed his name, loving every second of her orgasm as it washed over her.

When he was finished, he moved up, licking his lips. "I already have the tickets."

"What am I going to with you?" she asked.

"Marry me and love me."

"I suppose I can handle that."

The End

Out Now

USA Today Bestselling Authors
Sam Crescent Jenika Snow

PLAYER

A TABOO SHORT

Derek

I wasn't going to have her running from me about anything short of the truth. Yes, I'd fucked a great deal of the bitches from our school, but they had used me as much as I'd used them. It was a done deal between us all. I'd stopped fucking anyone since Charlotte, and I saw she wanted to believe me. There was a spark of doubt in her eyes, and I got it. I'd never been perfect, and before Charlotte, I'd have fucked five girls at that party, and still gone home with a different girl.

My dad hadn't been that strict growing up, and he wasn't now. He'd asked me to take Charlotte into consideration before bringing bitches home to screw. To be honest, he just didn't want to have to deal with her mother bitching at him. It was different for girls compared to boys. My father had even agreed that Charlotte wasn't allowed to bring boys home.

That was okay; there was a guy right here, right now, and he was already home, and she could do whatever the hell she wanted to do with him.

"You feel that, baby?" I asked, pushing my aching cock against her stomach.

She moaned and that turned me on even more.

"I want to fuck you so damn bad, and don't worry. I know it's your first time, and I'll be careful."

"What about our parents?" she asked, growling a little.

I smiled. "Who gives a fuck what they think? You and I both know we're not related. I've never once thought of you as my sister. Do you see me as your brother?"

"No."

"Then we've got nothing to lose. We're not breaking any fucking laws here, baby. They didn't think about us long enough to give a shit when they got married. Why should we give a shit now?"

When I'd found out that my father's latest piece of ass came with a kid, and not only was he fucking this one, he wanted to marry her, I'd been pissed. The moment I discovered my new sister would be Charlotte, I'd been so damned angry. She was the one girl at school I'd wanted and refused to approach. Lame, I know but that's the way it is.

She was the one girl I believed I couldn't have, the good girl, and then she was in my house, using my shower, and looking so fucking good all the time. I'd never taken the time to get to know her. Charlotte was simply one girl in my year, and that was all I knew about her.

I moved away from her, and removed my shirt so that she could get a good fucking look at what she would be turning down if she decided not to fuck me. Throwing the shirt aside, I cup her cheek and run my thumb across her bottom lip.

"Are you going to turn me down, baby? Your pussy is so damn wet; I can promise you, you'll love every single thing I do to you."

"What are you going to do?" she asked, licking those lips.

My cock was in fucking pain at being restrained in my jeans. I didn't like it.

"I'm going to get you naked and lay you on the edge of my bed." I leaned in and sucked her bottom lip into my mouth.

She gasped, arching up toward my touch.

"Then I'm going to lick your creamy cunt until you come all over my face." I smiled as she pressed a little closer to me.

I take a step back and loop my finger within her belt loops. "Are you going to get naked for me, baby? Are you going to play with me?"

Charlotte

"Yes."

Fuck, yes, I wanted to play. I wanted to get naked and have his mouth between my thighs. I'd never been with a guy before; Derek was the first guy who'd ever made me feel like this. I was so turned on that my pussy was slick and need consumed me.

He tugged me closer to him. "Take your clothes off."

Swallowing the lump in my throat, I stared into his normally cold eyes and was shocked by the heat inside them. He was enflamed, aroused, and all because of me. I should have been afraid and run from him, but I couldn't move away. He had hypnotized me to the spot. I tugged my shirt off and wriggled out of my jeans at the same time he rid himself of his jeans, my mouth going dry at the sight of *that*. He was huge. I mean, really big. Painfully big.

How was he even going to fit inside me?

I wasn't a small girl, but that thing wasn't normal.

He wrapped his hand around it and started pumping up and down the shaft. Pre-cum leaked out of the tip, slickening up his dick.

"You're not naked yet, Charlotte," he said.

Glancing down, I saw I had yet to remove my bra and panties. Reaching behind me, I unhooked the catch of my bra, and it sprang off my large breasts. Yes, I'd been blessed or cursed, whichever way you looked at it, with large boobs.

I pressed the bra against my body as the reality of our situation invaded once again. He'd been with so many girls; I was going to pale in comparison.

Suddenly, his hands were in front of me, capturing my wrists, and peeling my arms away from my body.

"You don't need to hide from me, baby." He pressed a sweet, tender kiss to my lips and proceeded to remove my bra and panties. Derek wrapped an arm around my waist and pulled me in closer to him. I took a deep breath as he surrounded me.

He moved me toward the edge of the bed, and I half expected him to throw me to the bed and pounce, but he didn't.

Derek captured my chin and forced me to look at him. "If at any time you want me to stop, just say so. I'm not into forcing women who don't want to be with me, understand."

"I understand."

"I want to make you feel good, nothing else."

"I know." One of the nicest things he'd said to me in a long time, he was reassuring me that it was going to be fine between us. If he were an asshole, would he do that?

I was starting to realize that there was so much more to Derek than I'd thought.

OUT NOW

Crescent Snow Publishing

More information on Sam Crescent and Jenika Snow's CSP titles can be found below:

www.CrescentSnowPublishing.com

Want to join the Crescent Snow Facebook Street Team?

Made in the USA
Middletown, DE
30 August 2016